Longarm heard a low, menacing growl, and realized he'd rolled onto one of the damn dogs. The dog had also bedded down for the night underneath the sheep wagon.

The dog's bite was more by way of warning than it was serious. The animal did not bother with Longarm further, but dashed out into the pitch-black night. Enough light came off a dying fire to show Longarm that when it ran, wherever it was going and for whatever reason, the dog's ears were forward and its tail was held high. Whatever was out there, the dog did not respond to the threat.

It should have, Longarm decided a moment later. The sound that had wakened him was repeated. It was a high-pitched, quavering yell. It was not particularly loud, but there was something about the shrill timbre of the sound that made it carry through the night.

TABOR EVANS

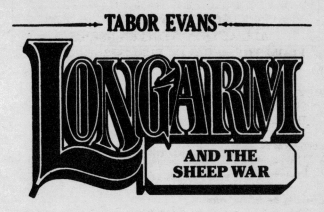

LONGARM
AND THE
SHEEP WAR

JOVE BOOKS, NEW YORK

LONGARM AND THE SHEEP WAR

A Jove Book / published by arrangement with
the author

PRINTING HISTORY
Jove edition / September 1999

The Penguin Putnam Inc. World Wide Web site address is
http://www.penguinputnam.com

ISBN: 0-515-12572-5

A JOVE BOOK®
Jove Books are published by The Berkley Publishing Group,
a division of Penguin Putnam Inc.,
375 Hudson Street, New York, New York 10014.
JOVE and the "J" design
are trademarks belonging to Penguin Putnam Inc.

PRINTED IN THE UNITED STATES OF AMERICA

10 9 8 7 6 5 4 3 2 1

Chapter 1

Custis Long, United States deputy marshal, whistled as he ambled along Denver's busy Colfax Avenue. He tipped his hat to a matron whose mustache was almost as full as his, then crossed the street and mounted the steps to the imposing gray stone structure of the Federal Building.

It was a fine, fair spring morning, and he felt good. Looked good too if he did say so, having just come from a barbershop where he'd treated himself to a trim, a splash of bay rum, and most important, a barber-chair shave. There was something about a barber shave that made the world seem a gentler and more pleasant place after leaving the chair than when entering it, and today was no different.

It was, however, somewhat unusual for Long to feel so full of himself. Generally speaking, he had some difficulty trying to comprehend just why the ladies fair seemed to find him so attractive. His own critical inspections when peering into mirrors failed to enlighten him.

What he saw there was ordinary and mundane in the extreme. He was tall, something over six feet in height, and had wide shoulders and a lean frame. His face was weather-worn and creased. His hair and handlebar mustache were a dark · seal-brown, and his eyes the same piercing gold-brown as an eagle's.

This afternoon he wore the flat-crowned brown Stetson that he favored, freshly blacked stovepipe cavalry boots, a brown tweed coat, tan corduroy trousers, and a calfskin vest buttoned over a brown check shirt and string tie.

As always, regardless of whatever else he might have chosen for the day, the use-worn grips of a double-action .44 Colt revolver rode on his belly just inches to the left of his belt buckle, its holster canted at a shallow angle for a quick draw.

Not that he expected to be challenged on a Denver sidewalk in the middle of a business day, but some habits were worth cultivating, and the ready presence of a pistol could be considered essential for any man in Long's line of employment.

He entered the Federal Building in no hurry whatsoever, then scowled after glancing at the wall clock in the foyer. It showed he was late by a good eight minutes. Not that U.S. Marshal Billy Vail really had any cause to expect punctuality from his top deputy—why create a precedent after all these years—but it peeved Long to judge the time so poorly as that.

He paused for a moment and dragged his railroad-grade Ingersoll watch from a vest pocket, then snorted and returned the turnip-shaped and ungainly, but impeccably accurate, instrument to his pocket.

"Henry," he declared as he swept into the chief marshal's outer office, "make a note to tell the building maintenance people that that damn clock is out of fix again. It's running nine minutes fast."

"They just fixed it last week," the marshal's mousy and bespectacled secretary returned.

"No, last week they thought they fixed it. Fact is, they didn't." Long tossed his Stetson onto a bare limb of the hat rack that stood in the corner.

"That could well be," Henry said, "but I happen to know that the boss set his watch to agree with that one just this morning."

"Is that a fact? Well, let me tell you—"

"Longarm!" a voice bellowed from beyond the closed door leading into Billy Vail's private office. "Is that you out there? Finally?"

Henry gave Longarm a sly grin, but stopped short of adding the almost obligatory "See, I told you so." But then that wasn't really necessary. Longarm winced. And tapped lightly on Billy Vail's door.

"I have a job for you."

Longarm grunted softly, giving his boss free rein to interpret the sound however he pleased. It wasn't as if the statement was a major pronouncement. There were only a limited number of reasons why Longarm would be summoned to Billy's office in the middle of a workday, and the handing out of assignments would be square on top of the list.

"You know Wyoming," Billy added.

Longarm looked up from the chore of cleaning his fingernails. "It's kinda big place, Billy. I wouldn't claim t' know all of it. Quite."

"Warren County," the balding, red-cheeked marshal said. Billy Vail looked something like a plump, aging cherub. Which was proof enough that looks could be deceiving. Before he'd accepted the largely administrative appointment as a chief marshal, this same innocent-appearing jasper had been a Texas Ranger. One of the best. He knew the rules and followed them, but within those boundaries he was tough, relentless, and when necessary deadly. Billy Vail knew the smell of gun smoke and the exhilaration of survival afterward. Longarm respected him greatly, and hoped the feeling was returned in kind.

"I'm told there's whole damn states back east that aren't as big as Warren County, Wyoming Territory," Longarm said.

"I'll check on that for you if you think it's important. You do know the country up there, I take it," Vail persisted.

Longarm shrugged, then reached into his coat for a cheroot and into his vest for a match. He took his time about nipping the tip off the cigar and lighting up. "I been through, o' course. A man almost has to if he's going from Cheyenne up to Deadwood or the Belle Fourche River country. I wouldn't say I know it particularly well, though."

"You're going to," the marshal informed him.

3

"Izzat so?"

"Yes, it is. In fact, I would say you are going to become intimately familiar with that part of Wyoming Territory." Billy commenced to grin. "One step at a time."

"You want to run that one by me again, Boss?"

Billy Vail ignored the question. Instead he turned his desk chair to the side and dropped his chin onto steepled fingertips for a minute or two. Then he turned back to face Longarm again. "How do you get along with sheep?" he asked.

"I'm not real fond o' mutton. Too strong for my taste. A rack o' lamb goes down pretty nice, though. An' I'd admit to owning a wool blanket. Does that count for anything?"

"If that is what we have, my friend, then that is what we shall work with." Billy's grin appeared positively diabolical to Longarm now.

"Boss, when you start callin' me friend—right here in the office an' no bartender in sight t' be asking for refills—I got to tell you it makes me kinda nervous."

"There's nothing for you to be nervous about, Longarm." The grin spread even wider. "Trust me."

"Hell, Billy, now I really *am* worried."

Chapter 2

Longarm was the last one off the train. He stepped down slowly, more than half hoping there would be no one left hanging around the platform to see him.

It wasn't that he was a vain man. Far from it. But dammit, some things were simply . . . undignified. And embarrassing. This here was one of them.

Generally tidy about his appearance, now Longarm looked—well, disheveled would have been a mild way to phrase it. Lousy would be somewhat more accurate. As in the literal definition by which a man of his appearance could reasonably be expected to harbor tiny livestock on his person.

Instead of his usual snuff-brown Stetson hat, he wore a battered and filthy old black Kossuth of ancient military vintage. Instead of tweeds and corduroy, he had on jeans so crusted with manure they were surely capable of standing—for that matter, maybe walking too—on their own. Instead of his customary shirt, tie, and vest, his torso was covered only with the faded and slightly tattered red flannel of a union suit. He had a black bandanna—cheaper than the more popular red or blue neck cloths—knotted at his throat, and his boots were rundown at the heels and looked as though they hadn't been blacked since the long-ago day when they were new.

In his belt he'd stuffed a revolver, but judging from its appearance there might well be question about whether the intended use of the weapon was to shoot with or to hammer nails. The grips were broken and partly missing, and a scrap of twine with no discernible purpose was knotted around the curve of the gun's hammer. Carried as it was in the front of his trousers, it looked as if he might be able to get the gun into action if given maybe a half hour or so of forewarning.

But then looks could at times be deceiving. The revolver was in fact Longarm's trusted .44 albeit with the usual grips replaced. And the twine indeed had no purpose save to convince observers that the owner of such a foul excuse for a weapon knew nothing about firearms.

Nor was the double-action Colt stuck quite so casually into Longarm's britches as he wanted others to believe. After he'd bought the ratty jeans from a friend who specialized in breaking horses for a living and who had wallowed the garment in the dirt and manure of many a corral, Longarm had taken them to a tailor and had a holster of soft, glove leather sewn into the waistband. The position and the angle of the revolver that rode there was exactly what Longarm was used to.

But he surely did look . . . lousy. Rather artfully so, if he did say so himself. Artfully and somewhat embarrassingly too.

He stepped onto the platform at the Cheyenne railroad depot, a burlap sack containing his worldly possessions in one hand, and looked around.

He was supposed to be met here. Billy Vail told him he would be. Billy'd had no idea what the contact would look like, just that his name was Rodrigo and that he would collect Longarm at the depot this afternoon.

Longarm reached for his watch. And remembered too late that he did not have it. The Ingersoll, along with the .44-caliber derringer that rode at the end of his watch chain, was back at his boardinghouse room in Denver, right along with his vest, his Stetson, his . . . He managed to keep from growling aloud, but only just.

The train had unloaded, taken on new passengers, and pulled away again sometime ago, leaving the platform empty except for a rather nattily dressed businessman who was still hanging about, probably waiting for a message at the adjacent telegraph office.

Longarm had no way to check the time on his own, so he left his bag lying where it was and stepped inside the depot. A Regulator wall clock showed that he had been waiting there the better part of a half hour.

Billy hadn't given any instructions as to what he should do if this Rodrigo failed to show. It was something neither of them had considered back in Denver. Longarm rather wished now that he'd thought to ask.

He looked at the clock, glanced back outside to the empty platform, and thought about waiting indoors. At least there were some benches inside the station building where he might sit.

Still, Billy's instructions were clear. Rodrigo was to meet him on the platform. Not inside the station, on the platform, dammit.

Longarm tried once more to look at his pocket watch, and cursing softly under his breath, settled for scratching his belly instead at the spot where a vest pocket should have been.

Not only was he having to stand around in public looking like a derelict, dammit, but now the businessman was staring at him.

With the sort of luck he was having today, Longarm thought he would be fortunate if the businessman didn't call a town constable and have the derelict taken away on suspicion of vagrancy or something.

The businessman appeared to be about as impatient as Longarm was commencing to feel. The fellow looked back and forth, up and down the tracks, but there was nothing to see out there except bare, empty steel. The train was long gone, and no other was scheduled to arrive for the better part of an hour. Longarm had noticed that on the board when he'd looked in to check the time.

The handsomely dressed businessman shifted nervously from one foot to another. He pulled a watch from his pocket and glanced at the time. Looked as if he was going to walk away, then turned back with stiff, angry body movement. Longarm sympathized. He knew how the man felt.

After dithering for several long moments, the man seemed to summon his nerve. He marched across the platform and stopped before Longarm.

"I, um, there is something I would like to ask you. It may sound strange. And I don't mean to be rude. But . . . well . . . do you mind?"

The businessman had a very faint accent. Longarm could not place it, though. Spanish? French? Perhaps Italian? Definitely not German or Russian or any of those. He wasn't sure what it was.

"Well?" the businessman asked.

Longarm blinked. "Oh. Uh. No, I reckon I don't mind. You ask whatever you like."

The fellow looked around as if afraid of being overheard. "Your name would not happen to be Long, would it?"

Longarm rolled his eyes. "Rodrigo?"

The businessman broke into a huge, relieved grin. "You *are* Long!"

"And you're Rodrigo."

"I was expecting someone dressed . . . how shall I say this?"

Longarm laughed. "Yeah, well, I was expecting to meet someone who looked like a sheepherder."

Rodrigo chuckled. "Just as I expected to meet someone who looks like a marshal."

Longarm grinned, tried to reach into a coat pocket that wasn't there, and remembered to pull off his misshapen old hat, that being the only place he could think of in this get-up to carry his cheroots and matches. He offered one to Rodrigo and selected another for himself.

"Pleased t' meet you," Longarm said, meaning it.

8

"And I am most pleased to meet you." Rodrigo bent and picked up Longarm's sack of possibles, which turned out to be heavy with spare ammunition. "Shall we go, Marshal? We should find a place where we can talk in private, no?"

"Sounds fine. But call me Longarm, Rodrigo. All my friends do."

Together, the impeccably attired sheepherder and the scarecrow figure who was Billy Vail's best U.S. deputy marshal left the Cheyenne railroad station.

Chapter 3

Rodrigo turned out to be the businessman's last name, not his first as Longarm had surmised. He was Jorge Luis Rodrigo, he said as they walked along Front Street to a small office located in an alley close to the Union Pacific shipping pens. Gilt lettering on a glass panel in the door stated that the office housed the Smith, Williams, and Winton Land and Livestock Company, Inc.

"I don't understand," Longarm admitted. "I thought Billy told me you're the owner of the outfit. So who are Smith, Williams, and Winton?"

Rodrigo laughed. "Nice Anglo-sounding names, are they not? At least I thought so when I picked them. And not such a giveaway as Smith and Jones, I think?"

"You mean there ain't any . . .?"

Rodrigo's face split into a broad, happy grin. "There is just me." •

"Land and Livestock?" Longarm inquired.

"There is land. Leased, of course, or free range. But there has to be land."

"And the livestock?"

"Ah, livestock we have, yes. But not the cattle such a name might imply. Sheep, Marshal. Many, many sheep." He shrugged. "But why advertise, eh? There are enough who know the truth. I don't want to ask for trouble from any more than are necessary."

The businessman—and he was indeed a man of business, Longarm was quickly concluding—hunted on a ring of keys for the proper one that would admit them into the Smith, Williams, and Winton offices, then opened the door and motioned for Longarm to enter.

The office was small and cluttered. There were several maps and some stylized pictures of chunky Hereford cattle displayed on the walls. Nowhere in sight was there anything that would hint of sheep. Jorge Rodrigo was a cautious man indeed.

Rodrigo closed the door behind him and motioned his guest to one of the two chairs in the place, then seated himself behind a desk piled high with papers.

"Is all of that . . . ?" Longarm motioned toward the clutter of forms, fliers, and old newspapers.

"Unimportant," Rodrigo confirmed. "If it is all stolen or burned or whatever, there is no loss. The documents that are important to me are in a fireproof safe—never mind where that is—or are kept in a safe deposit box at my bank."

Longarm nodded. He was deciding that he liked and rather respected this sheepman.

"Billy said you could fill me in on the problem you're having up here. All I know is that it's taken place on land you lease from the Lakota nation, an' that gives us jurisdiction."

Rodrigo frowned and spread his hands as if in apology. "That, um, may well be true."

"May be?"

"Or, uh, may not be. I am not certain of this. Which I was very clear about when I discussed the matter with the Indian agent."

"Will Hancock?" Longarm guessed.

"Yes, do you know him?"

"We're old friends." He smiled. "It also kinda explains how I got inta this. Will and me think alike. We . . . how ought

11

I put this? Neither one of us wants t' see damnfoolery get in the way o' justice."

"Foolery like . . . ?"

It was Longarm's turn to grin. "Oh, stuff like petty interpretation of rules an' regulations. Will and me think the spirit o' the law is sometimes as important as the letter."

"I think I understand. Yes, your Mr. Hancock can be like that. This much I had heard about him. And yes, it was he who brought up your name. He, uh, he suggested that since there are no precisely marked boundaries, it is entirely possible that some of my problems have taken place on reservation lands. Or, um, perhaps not. In any event this attitude of his, which I understand you to share, is one of the reasons I chose to approach him after . . . other recourse failed."

"An' what recourse might that've been, Jorge? Can I call you Jorge, by the by?"

"Please do."

"An' I'm Longarm to my friends."

"Then Longarm and Jorge it shall be, my friend."

"You were sayin' something about looking for help elsewhere before you talked to Will about your problem?"

"That is correct. I take it you are acquainted with Warren County?"

"Some. Not real well, but some."

"You know that the county seat is a town called McCollum."

"Yes, sir."

"And the sheriff is a man named Michael Bennett."

"That I didn't know, but I reckon I can take your word on it."

"Believe me, I wish I could tell you something else, but this Mr. Bennett is unfortunately the sheriff. It was to him that I turned for help the first four, five, six times my people had problems."

"I gather he didn't do you no good."

"You gather correctly, sir. Oh, he put on a fine show of cooperation. He took me into his office and brought an aman-

12

uensis in to record my statement. He had everything duly recorded and signed. With witnesses, I must say, and a notary. It was all quite official.''

"And then?" Longarm suspected he could guess how that would be answered, but he needed to ask it anyway.

"And then . . . nothing. Oh, if you were to ask him, I am certain the good sheriff will be able to recite for you chapter and verse on the law governing the use of free-range grasslands. And those laws pertaining to the protection of life and property. I suspect he could also tell you, perhaps even show you written records to prove his deputies expended many hours of effort trying to locate the people who have been marauding on the public lands.''

"Marauding," Longarm repeated. "What exactly d'you mean by that?"

"At first they only issued warnings. Then they scattered the flocks. Then they shot some of my sheep. Then they shot many of my sheep. The last straw was when they murdered one of my employees. He was only a boy.'' Rodrigo frowned. "Do you know the Basque people, Longarm?"

Longarm shook his head. "Not well. Heard of them, of course.''

"I rely on them. They are good people. Tenacious and dependable, and they know sheep. I am Portuguese myself. You thought Mexican perhaps?"

Longarm didn't say anything. Hell, he hadn't actually given that question much thought. It wasn't of particular concern to him. Might've been to some, he supposed, but he didn't much care where a man hailed from or what he looked like, but what the man was like on the inside.

"I have known of the Basques all my life. They are proud people. Independent. And they can be fierce. They are patient, Longarm my friend, but they are not known to be forgiving. If the people who hate me—hate my sheep, I should say—if these people want to create a war, they will continue to offend the Basques. You have heard of the blood feuds in your West Virginia?" Rodrigo asked.

13

"That's the part o' the country I'm originally from myself," Longarm admitted.

Rodrigo nodded. "Then you know," he said.

"I know."

"I will tell you something, my new and disreputable-looking friend."

"What's that, Jorge?"

"If these Basques lose patience and declare for the blood of the men behind these evil things, your West Virginia family feuds will seem no worse than a squabble among children at play in the schoolyard."

"I'm kinda surprised you'd care so much about the fate o' whoever's been killing your livestock, Jorge."

"Longarm my friend, it is not the guilty ones whose lives I would fear for, but all the innocents who might die with them. If the Basques call in the clans, my friend, there is no guarantee how much blood would fertilize the grass before they would see it as enough."

"You're sayin' we could have a war on our hands here, Jorge?"

"Worse than any the Lakota ever waged. An Indian can be placated, Longarm. Talk peace with him, smoke the pipe with him, he will believe what you say and trust you to keep your word. He will agree to stop fighting, at least until the next time. But a Basque washes his honor clean only in the blood of his enemies. With him there can be no peace so long as one enemy still lives. One enemy or any member of that enemy's family. You know what I am saying?"

Longarm whistled. "I reckon you'd best fill me in on what you an' Will had in mind when you asked me t' come up here."

14

Chapter 4

"Care for a smoke?" Longarm asked with a smile. Emil looked at him, blinked, and looked forward again over the rumps of the two short-coupled cobs that were pulling the resupply wagon. Longarm had no idea if Emil spoke English or not. So far the man hadn't spoken a word of any sort, not one since they'd pulled out of Cheyenne. And that had been— he would have checked his watch for the time except he didn't have the damn thing—hours ago. He wasn't sure how many. Hours. That was as close as he could figure it.

The idea was that Emil was to take him out to where one of the flocks was being held on grazing ground north of Cheyenne. Longarm was to hook up there with the herder, a man by the name of Paolo. Then Longarm would go along as swamper, cook, or general slave. The details about what an observer might assume was Longarm's job didn't really matter, as the point was to put Longarm out there with the sheep where he could keep an eye on whatever happened to them on their way through Warren County into South Dakota. Or maybe it was northern Nebraska. The specifics of geography tended to become fuzzy when a fellow was walking across several hundred miles of roadless, unfenced grass.

And that, of course, was very good so far as Will Hancock's idea went. His reasoning was that since no one was positive

15

the past crimes took place in Warren County, Wyoming Territory, then it was entirely possible—likely even, if a person wanted to argue for it strongly enough—that the depredations occurred on Lakota tribal lands. And if they took place on tribal land, why, federal authority prevailed and one deputy marshal named Custis Long could assume jurisdiction regardless of what Sheriff Michael Bennett said, did, or wanted.

That, at least, was the theory.

Hell, it was good enough by Longarm's reckoning too. Any lawyers who wanted to toss their two cents worth in were welcome to do so. But after the fact, thank you, and not until Longarm put a stop to the sheep-cow problems before they turned into an undeclared war.

Jorge Rodrigo's wagon driver, Emil, wasn't much for idle chitchat, but there was nothing wrong with his sense of direction. He took the wagon straight as a string across bare, only slightly rolling terrain, until Longarm himself wasn't sure just exactly where they were.

He was reasonably certain they were still west of the Mississippi and south of the Missouri. Beyond that, he was not willing to declaim.

Just short of noon, though, judging by the sun over Longarm's shoulder, they topped a small rise and came rattling and clattering down into a pocket seemingly filled with crackwillow and a carpet of white wildflowers.

Except on closer inspection the white wasn't flowers at all, but an immense and sprawling flock of woolies, and the brush wasn't low-growing willow or wild plum after all, but a stand of full-grown cottonwoods.

The distances and perspective had been such that even with his years on the prairie to draw from, Longarm had been fooled into thinking they were closer than they were when they topped that rise.

He thought about complimenting Emil on his navigation, decided there was no point in it, and remained silent the rest

of the still-considerable distance into this one of Jorge Rodrigo's many sheep camps.

"Thank you," Longarm said as he dropped off of the wagon
box and reached into the bed for the sack that held his things.
"Gracias," he added. *"Grazie.* Uh, *tak. Danke."*

"You're quite welcome. Any time," Emil responded. And
burst out laughing.

Longarm wondered if this was typical of the Basque sense
of humor. He also wondered if anyone would mind if he
punched Emil vigorously in the mouth just one time.

Dammit, though. Longarm's mustache commenced to
quiver, and in another few moments he was laughing too. At
himself. "You got me," he confessed when he could draw
breath enough for it.

Emil's eyes sparkled with good humor. "I'd take that cigar
now if you was to offer one again."

Longarm pulled out two, trimmed his own, and lighted both
of them when Emil was ready.

"Come along," the wagon driver said. "You need to meet
Paolo."

Longarm was eager for that and was, he thought, prepared
to make the acquaintance of another short, swarthy, rough-
dressed man pressed from pretty much the same mold as Emil.

He was not prepared for the person who stepped out of the
sheep wagon parked close to a tiny creek that seemed to take
its head somewhere in the cottonwood grove here.

The person who stepped out to greet them surely could not
be named Paolo, Longarm reasoned.

She was small. She was dark. She was swarthy. She had a
woman's miniature figure grafted onto a child-sized body. She
had gleaming black hair that was gathered into a thick rope
of braid. Even when shortened by the braiding, her hair hung
well below waist level.

Not that that meant it was so long, though, Longarm reflected. Little-bitty as this woman was, it didn't take much to
reach from her head down to her waist. He doubted she would

17

come higher than his breastbone if she stood against him.

Not that he wanted to hold on to her anyway. She wasn't pretty. She had a sharp jawline and a nose like a hawk's beak. She had eyebrows like two woolly caterpillars perched on her face, and lips that were too big surrounding a mouth that was enough for a woman twice her size.

No, she wasn't at all pretty, Longarm reminded himself.

Then he paused to wonder just why it was that he was paying such damn close attention to a woman who wasn't pretty.

Striking, he decided. Probably because of her dress, which was a colorful—if not to say downright gaudy—skirt and blouse combination that practically screamed out loud with bold red, bright yellow, and a shade of green so bilious it could likely make a man puke if he'd had half a drink too many.

That was it, of course. It was the clothes that were striking, the wild-colored skirt and that lemon-colored blouse that hung off her shoulders and scooped low in front so the upper slopes of her tits were laid out for the world to admire.

Not that Longarm was interested in looking. Not in the slightest. No, sir.

"Long? Mister. Are you all right?" Emil tugged at the elbow of his union suit, and Longarm realized that the wagon driver had spoken to him a couple times already, a fact he was only just now beginning to register.

"Yeah, sure. What d'you want, Emil?"

"This girl, she is Paolo's daughter, Paula." Emil and the girl exchanged greetings, or whatever, in a language Longarm did not pretend to recognize. Then Emil turned back to Longarm.

"Paula, she says I should tell you she is sorry that her father is not here."

Longarm involuntarily glanced around. Except for this little oasis of sheep and shade, he was fairly sure there wasn't anyplace to wander off to in half a day's ride. And he and Emil had just come from a long way off without seeing anyone along the trail.

"Paolo had, shall we say, an errand to perform," Emil said.

"Anything I oughta know about?" Longarm asked.

Emil grinned. "There are certain supplies that our employer Mr. Rodrigo does not supply to us. If you take my meaning."

Longarm smiled back at the little man. "Kinda like the medicinal spirits I got in my bag here?" he suggested.

"A man can never be too cautious," Emil agreed. "Snakes, they are everywhere."

"Right." Longarm looked at the girl again. She still wasn't pretty, but dammit, she wasn't quite as ugly up close as he'd thought at first glance, and she seemed to be getting better looking even as he stood there; if this kept up she was gonna be a beauty before they got onto the Lakota reservation. He took his hat off and dropped his chin in a sort of bow. "Ma'am."

"It's miss, if you please," she said in clear, unaccented English.

Papa and maybe Mama too might well be Basque, Longarm thought, but this girl was American born and raised. He could hear that plain in her voice.

"Do we call you Mr. Long? Or Marshal?" she asked.

"Longarm will do. It's what all my friends use."

"Very well, Marshal. As you wish."

Had she been able to read in his eyes that first reaction to how kinda homely she was? He hoped not. Hell, he didn't want to be rude.

"Ma'am," he repeated in a dry tone. If the girl wanted to be contrary, well, she didn't own any exclusive rights to the notion.

Instead of bristling, though, Paula's eyes twinkled, and faint crow's-feet of amusement appeared at their outer corners. "I think we will get along just fine, Marshal," she announced, stepping forward and offering a hand for him to shake.

Chapter 5

"Leave the supplies under the wagon, Emil." Paula paused for a moment to give Longarm a thorough looking-over. "I hope you brought plenty of extra."

"I did," Emil said.

"Good. Help yourselves to lunch then." Without another word the girl picked up a battered slide-action .22 rifle, which had been leaning against a wheel of the narrow, canvas-roofed sheepherders wagon, and walked away. As soon as she moved past the campfire that smoldered inside a ring of stones, a fuzzy black-and-white dog darted out from beneath the wagon to take up a station at her heels.

Longarm noticed several other similar dogs lolling about on the fringes of the flock of sheep. None of them looked as if they would weigh more than thirty pounds or so. They seemed a collection of small and rather scruffy mutts. He was not impressed by them. Their mistress, on the other hand . . .

"She's leaving?" he asked.

"I think she left already," Emil said.

"But what about lunch?"

"If you are hungry, eat."

"But . . ."

"You don't cook? I brought cans. Fruits, beans, like that. You want a can of something?"

"I just kinda assumed, with a woman in the camp an' all . . ."

Emil chuckled. "Paula, she is not a woman."

Longarm gave Emil a laugh and a wink. "In that case, friend, he damn sure fooled me."

"You know she is a woman, Long. I know it. I think even her papa suspects it. But Paula, she does not know."

"I see," Longarm said, not entirely sure that he did.

"You want a can of beans? I know right where they are."

"No, I'll . . . you got bacon? Flour? Saleratus?"

"Sure. I brought them and lard too. You making hoecakes?"

"Stick bread."

"Same thing. Make enough for two, will you? I'll unload while you cook. Here." Emil dug into the back of his supply wagon for the things Longarm wanted, then turned the cooking chores over to the tall deputy and gave his own attention to the unloading of supplies for what was now the trio of sheepherders who would be grazing this flock all the way to the Lakota tribal lands.

Longarm rolled out of his blankets with his Colt in hand. He rolled hard onto something soft and warm and yielding.

Before he had time to figure out what it was that snapped him out of sleep, he felt a sharp, raking sting on the wrist that was hard enough that he nearly dropped the revolver. "What the . . ."

He heard a low, menacing growl, and realized he'd rolled onto one of the damn dogs. The dog had also bedded down for the night underneath the sheep wagon.

The dog's bite was more by way of warning than it was serious. The animal did not bother with Longarm further, but dashed out into the pitch-black night. Enough light came off a dying fire to show Longarm that when it ran, wherever it was going and for whatever reason, the dog's ears were forward and its tail was held high. Whatever was out there, the dog did not respond as if to a threat.

21

It should have, Longarm decided a moment later. The sound that had wakened him was repeated. It was a high-pitched, quavering yell. It was not particularly loud, but there was something about the shrill timbre of the sound that made it carry through the night.

Overhead, inside the sheep wagon, Longarm could hear small thumping and bumping. Apparently Paula had been wakened by this intrusion too. Longarm shoved his Colt back into its holster, and clambered out from under the wagon in time to see the door swing open. Paula stepped outside, and Longarm found himself wishing for more firelight. She was wearing what looked like a discarded shirt, a man-sized garment that engulfed her narrow shoulders and covered her to about mid-thigh, leaving most of her legs exposed.

Damn nice legs, Longarm saw. A trifle skinny. But shapely enough. They were that, all right.

Those rather nice legs ended at the lower parts inside a pair of loose, mud-crusted half-boots that the girl must have stepped into when she woke.

But then, Longarm realized, sheepherders likely were all too accustomed to being roused out of a sound sleep by emergencies of one sort or another. Probably they learned to go to bed prepared for the possibility of having to jump up and run.

Longarm still had no idea what the emergency was this time, but both the dog and Paula seemed prepared to meet it.

Longarm rubbed sleep out of his eyes, and bent to fumble around until he could locate a cheroot. Back in Denver Billy Vail had suggested to him that a down-on-his-luck sheepherder's helper would not be able to afford the expensive nickel cigars that Longarm favored. He'd said perhaps his deputy should outfit himself—at government expense, of course—with a box of rum crooks for the trip instead.

"Dammit, Billy, if anybody asks what I paid for my smokes, I'll just lie, all right? Better yet, I'll tell 'em I stole the things. But don't ask me t' give up my cheroots. I'd do a lot in the name o' justice, Billy, but a man has t' have some limits about how far he'll degrade himself.''

Longarm had brought a supply of cheroots for this trip. Now he felt that he needed one. He went over to the fire and used a wisp of grass ignited on the coals to light his smoke, then took advantage of the firelight to inspect his wrist where the damn dog had nipped him. There was a streak of red to show where the teeth had raked him, but the skin was not broken.

Longarm stood, his knee joints creaking, and the odd, piercing call was repeated from the darkness.

Paula startled the hell out of Longarm by tilting her head back and emitting an identical screech of her own. Well, close enough to it for Longarm's mind.

Apparently satisfied then, the girl came over to the fire and began adding wood to it. Longarm stepped back. It wasn't that he minded the heat, but the light directly in front of the girl turned the cloth of her nightshirt a translucent yellow and caught the outline of her body in sharp silhouette.

When she turned just a mite, he could see quite as clearly as if she'd been naked the small but tidy shape of her left tit and the tiny cone of nipple that perched on top of it. There wasn't much there. But what there was was choice.

Longarm looked at the girl's face. And discovered her looking right back into his eyes.

"Satisfied?" she asked.

"With what?" His voice was syrupy with innocence. He'd been caught looking, all right. But he didn't have to admit to it.

Paula rolled her eyes. Then she laughed softly and said, "Fill the coffeepot, will you? The water barrel is on the other side of the wagon."

"You're going to make coffee at this hour?"

"I will if you'll bring me the water like I asked you to. Or do you want me to go get it myself?"

Longarm picked up the pot from beside the fire ring and went to fetch the damn water.

The girl in the meantime, he saw, was breaking out the skillet he'd used to cook their supper the previous evening.

It seemed on the early side of things for breakfast, he thought. But then what the hell did he know about how to run a sheep camp?

Chapter 6

Paolo Laxha was a very happy man. Also a very drunk one. Longarm didn't know just how his daughter had known he was on his way in, but she had, and the coffee was nearly ready by the time Paolo stumbled into camp. The man was barefoot, his black hair was in wild disarray, and he looked like a man who had been on a week-long drunk. Which quite possibly he had, Longarm reflected.

For reasons best known to himself, Paolo had chosen to lead his mule rather than ride it home.

Of course it could very well be that the man was afraid of heights. The mule was huge, a mighty fine-looking animal indeed, and as tall as any Longarm had ever seen.

As man and beast came nearer to the fire, Longarm could see why Paolo had chosen to walk instead of ride. There wasn't room on the big animal's back for anyone to sit. All the available space was already occupied. By two wooden crates that looked suspiciously like the sort of thing bonded whiskeys were shipped in.

Then the mule turned sideways a little, and Longarm could read the lettering stenciled onto the sides of the crates. "Taylor and Boone, Rye Whiskey, Luciasport, Maryland."

Longarm began to grin. Paolo Laxha was surely a man after his own heart. Custis Long had surely come home.

Not that either Laxha or his daughter was paying any particular attention to their guest's sudden pleasure. Paula hurried to place a plate of something into her father's hands, then took the lead rope of the mule and led the animal off into the darkness.

Paolo hunkered silently by the fire and started in on the plate, which contained a rather unsavory-appearing mound of rice darkened by liberal helpings of black beans, bits of unidentifiable meat—unidentifiable at least to Longarm—and assorted other chunks and pieces that might have been vegetable in nature. Or not. In all, the heap of stuff looked rather nasty, Longarm thought. But it smelled damn well divine. It wouldn't have hurt his feelings any had the girl offered him some.

She hadn't, though, and that was that. Longarm stepped closer to the fire, and poured a cup of coffee for Paolo and another for himself.

Paolo said something to him in whatever language it was that Basques speak. Longarm could only look at him and shrug.

"I asked who da hell are you," Paolo tried in English.

"Oh. I'm your new helper."

Paolo gave him a plainly skeptical look, then shook his head.

"No?" Longarm asked.

"Bah. You? I don't t'ink so."

"Why the hell not?" Longarm demanded.

"You got da clothes right, mister, but you don' got da look of no sheep wagon fetch'um boy. Dat haircut, you got dat from some barber someplace. Don' lie to me, no. You pay more for dat haircut dan a sheep swamper make inna week. An' no sheep swamper gonna waste the money on no haircut. Your eyes, dey ain't right neither. Sheep boy, he got da strong back an' da weak head. You know? I see in you eyes you ain't like dat. Not you, no, sir. So what da hell you doin' here nohow?"

Longarm laughed. And introduced himself properly.

26

"Ah. Now dat make sense. You hide out here, den see what dem bad boys come do."

Longarm nodded. "That's about it in a nutshell, yes, sir."

"All right den. If Jorge say you belong, den you belong. Dat's fine. Just you stay outa da way. Don't mess wid da sheep an' don' mess wid da dogs."

"I notice you didn't say anything about me staying away from the mule or your daughter," Longarm said with a smile as Paolo shoveled one loaded spoon of the savory concoction after another past a curtain of mustache hair and into his mouth.

Paolo laughed so hard he almost choked, and had to swig a gulp of coffee to clear his throat before he could speak again. "You do what you want 'bout dem two. If you brave enough. Dat mule, stranger come 'round him he kick de man head off if he don' like dat fella. Paula, you gotta be even braver if you mess wid her, mister. Da mule only kick de head off. Paula, she don' like you she kick you balls off. Poof! One kick. You sing like little birdie in da nest." Paolo grinned and offered a high-pitched sample rendition by way of demonstration.

"I'll stay away from the sheep and the dogs," Longarm promised solemnly. That limited statement brought Paolo into new paroxysms of laughter.

"Tell you what, mister."

"I'd rather you call me Longarm. All my friends do."

Paolo nodded. "All right. I tell you what, Longarm my new friend an' now my wagon swamper. I want you should go find where my daughter put dat whiskey, eh? You bring one bottle back here, you and me gonna find out if it da right stuff. Okay by you?"

"That's sounds plenty okay by me."

It was, they subsequently determined after slow and meticulous examination, indeed the right stuff.

Chapter 7

"Hey, you, mister."

Longarm gave the girl a bleary-eyed, blinking look. Last night had been wet, and the morning was still mighty early. The sun hadn't yet made a personal appearance, although the horizon had taken on a rosy pink color that said the daily event would not be long in coming.

"That fire is good enough. Are you really going to help around the camp?"

"Yeah, I reckon so." Apart from the fact that anyone who chanced by shouldn't see anything questionable—a camp swamper who idled about in the shade while the Basques worked would certainly be deemed questionable, Longarm figured—Longarm would have gone quite thoroughly nuts if he had to spend the entire trip with nothing to do. And there were no guarantees they would encounter any trouble this time out. Rodrigo had admitted that he never knew when, where, or how often his flocks would encounter the marauders.

"Don't put the rest of that wood on the fire, mister. Throw it in the sling under the wagon," Paula ordered. "Then go hitch the mule."

"We're pulling out?"

She gave him a look of sorrowful exasperation. "You can be real slow sometimes, can't you, mister."

"I'll go hitch the mule," Longarm said. The damned girl was, he had to admit, right about that.

He took the chunks of age-dried dead wood he'd been carrying, and returned them to the canvas possum hanging underneath the sheepherders' wagon, being careful to make no noise. He didn't want to disturb Paolo. The poor little man had been knee-walking drunk a couple hours earlier when Longarm had helped him into the wagon. Longarm suspected Paolo would require most of the day to sleep off a drunk like that one. And when he did wake up, Longarm hoped Paolo's head was banging as bass-drum loud as Longarm's was right now. It would serve the little bastard right for being so free with his liquor.

Longarm yawned and stretched and eyed the mule, grazing about forty or fifty yards south of the cottonwood grove. The sheep were spread out like a dirty white blanket along the creek bank to the east.

Longarm distinctly remembered being warned about the mule's sometimes belligerent disposition. Likely the girl wanted to see if the animal would whack their guest. Just to start her day with a good laugh. And if pressed, Longarm would have had to admit that he was more than a trifle curious about that too. Mules were smart. But also cantankerous and contrary when the mood struck them. If Longarm remembered correctly through the fog of last night's rye whiskey, though, Paolo had said this particular critter only tried to kill people it didn't like, and if that was the case, then now would be a good time to see how Longarm rated.

He found harness and collar freshly oiled and neatly laid on the floor of the wagon's driving box. He took a moment to light that delicious first cigar of the day, then gathered up the gear and sauntered out to the mule.

Damn thing was grazing free, he saw as he came closer. There was no sign of hobbles or a picket rope to keep the animal from bolting away, and to Longarm's certain knowledge there was nothing to the south to block his escape until he got to, oh, probably the tollgate on the Raton Pass road.

He wouldn't encounter that for three hundred miles or so if he chose to run. And hell, at that it would be closer than the next barrier east, west, or north. Longarm rather hoped Paolo and Paula knew what to expect from this animal.

He took a few puffs on his cheroot and let the harness trail from his hand, allowing the mule plenty of time to see and to know what was expected. Obviously this animal did not hate being harnessed or it wouldn't be grazing loose, and Longarm's experience was that it was more often surprise that got a man in trouble with an animal than anything else. So he let the mule see what was coming and ambled ahead.

He was perfectly well aware that behind him, Paula had stopped whatever it was she was doing at the fire and was watching to see how the new swamper got along with the livestock.

Pretty damned well as it turned out. Longarm walked up beside the mule and took a few moments to scratch its poll and rub its neck, then slipped the bridle and bit into place and began draping the harness over its back, tugging and straightening and trying to figure out just exactly what went where.

The mule stood calm and easy and never offered to kick. For which Longarm was well and truly grateful.

He managed to get everything strapped and buckled where he thought it probably went, then picked up one of the coiled driving lines and led the mule back to the wagon.

Paula was openly staring.

"Something wrong?" he asked.

"You surprise me, that's all."

"How so?"

"Ichabod hates almost everybody."

"Ichabod?"

"Sure. Tall, big head on a skinny neck. It seemed to fit."

"I see," he said, not at all sure that he did. "Whatever. Your papa never said anything about Ichabod being quite that particular."

Paula grinned. "And ruin a perfectly good show?"

"Yeah, well, it's good enough then that it didn't happen or he would've slept through it anyhow."

Paula gave Longarm an odd look, then turned and pointed. Away down the shallow valley there was enough daylight now for Longarm to dimly make out the figure of a man striding along beside the flock of sheep. Wispy, ghostlike shadows seemed to flit and dart near him. It took Longarm a minute to recognize that the man most surely had to be Paolo—not passed out in the wagon but up and working before Longarm rolled out of his blankets—and that the barely visible small figures around him were the dogs. Man and dogs seemed to be herding the flock to the creek so the sheep could water.

"He'll come in when breakfast is ready," the girl explained.

Resilient little bastard, Longarm observed with no small degree of envy. The man obviously had a constitution tougher than saddle leather. "Reckon I'll go finish my chores now," was all Longarm could think of to say. He led the mule on to the wagon, and got busy hitching it between the shafts so they would be ready to roll whenever Paolo gave the word.

Chapter 8

The business of herding sheep was . . . boring, actually.

Eye-glazing, mind-numbing, foot-aching *boring*.

They crawled out of the sack before dawn, ate quickly—
Longarm couldn't see what all the damned rush was about,
but that was the way Paolo and Paula did it—and began moving the sheep north just as soon as the flock was done with
the morning watering.

Come noon they stopped, had a light, cold lunch that required no fire, and then moved on again.

Late in the afternoon they stopped, watered the sheep, and
circled them onto a bedground before the humans ate—a real
meal this time, cooked and everything—and then went to bed.
Alone. Paolo and Paula retreating to their bunks inside the
odd, barrel-like wagon that was their home, and Longarm underneath the wagon with nothing but a dog for company.

Exciting it was not.

Boring it was. And damn-all tiring because the entire jour-
ney was being undertaken on foot, at least as far as Longarm
was concerned. Paolo and Paula took turns walking behind the
slowly moving sheep, spelling each other off with stints driving Ichabod and the wagon. Longarm, on the other hand, had
to walk the distance.

He didn't mind walking. Usually. This effort seemed rather too much of an otherwise good thing, however. And damn but it was boring.

As for the sheepherders, he suspected they should be bored senseless too because even when they were working, they were not the ones doing the actual work. All they did was wave and whistle, and the quick, scampering dogs did all the herding that was necessary.

Longarm had no idea how the dogs knew what was required, the signals seeming to have no logical design, although obviously it was all entirely clear to the Basques and to the dogs alike. In a manner of speaking, he supposed, it was like a different language, and just because Longarm couldn't speak Polish, that didn't mean that a Pole couldn't. Same thing here, he gathered, except practically none of this language was spoken. It was all hand movement, whistles, tongue clicks, and an occasional bark or chirp. And that was from the people. The dogs said even less than that.

But they did get the job done. They darted and dashed, nipping at the hocks of any damnfool sheep that did not immediately respond to their control.

A wave of Paolo's hand could send two or three of the dogs racing to the front of the flock to swing the leaders to one side or another, taking the sheep exactly where and how Paolo wanted them. And while those dogs were busy at the head of the flock, the others would be just as attentive at the rear and along the sides, making sure none of the sheep lagged too far behind, keeping the shape of the flock tight and tidy while they were moving, and allowing them to spread only so far apart when they were allowed to stop and graze.

There were, Longarm eventually counted, eight dogs in all. One, very gray around the muzzle, stayed close to the wagon even during the day, and rarely ventured as far out as the sheep were kept. That one—a retiree, Longarm gathered—was even allowed to ride in the wagon through the heat of the afternoons. The younger and more athletic dogs handled the work, all of them busy while the flock was in motion, several of them at a time being allowed to come into camp at night to eat and rest before resuming their duties.

Except for the old dog, Longarm couldn't begin to tell them apart. Didn't much want to either. They were not a friendly bunch, not pets or play-pretties by any stretch of the imagination. Paolo and Paula seemed to like them just fine. Longarm couldn't figure out why, but they did.

"I think the old dog is starting to like me," Longarm commented on their third night out.

"Why is dat, hey?"

"She's sleeping next to me."

Paolo laughed. "She don't like you, Longarm. She just too damn stubborn to give up her spot. You sleepin' where she lak to be. Dat her place, 'at's all."

"Shit, just when I was starting to like her too."

"You 'member what I tol' you. Jus' leave be them sheep and 'em dogs an' you be all right."

Longarm glanced across the fire, off in the direction where Paula was hunkered down messing with something in a wooden bucket. She was facing away, and the posture presented a tight and nicely rounded little ass on view.

Paolo had warned him off the dogs and the sheep, but had said he was welcome to take his own chances with Paula and Ichabod. Well, Longarm was getting along with Ichabod just fine. He wondered . . .

Longarm looked back at Paolo. The little sheepherder was grinning from ear to ear.

Caught, dammit, Longarm conceded, a small amount of heat commencing to gather in the vicinity of his ears. Caught staring at Paula's ass. That would have been all right except, well, she *was* the man's daughter.

"I tol' you, friend. You mess wid dat old dog Queenie, you gonna get bit. You mess wid dat girl, you gonna get worse dan jus' bit. But you do what you wan' to, you hear? My Paula, she take care o' herself."

"I haven't forgot."

Paolo was still grinning. "It get too awful bad, Longarm, you tell me. I have dem dogs bring in a nice li'l ewe. Take her out in de dark. Take care o' you problem, right? Hell, I even loan you some big boots. Loose at de top, see. Stick dem hind leg down inside so dey hol' de sheep where you want 'er. An' don' you worry. I pick you out one very nice sheep. Virgin, she." The little man got to laughing so hard he practically doubled over and had to clutch at his belly to make the hurting stop.

"I'll let you know," Longarm said dryly.

The awkward thing, though, was that Paolo was joking about that. Or . . . was he?

Longarm didn't honestly know, what with all the things a man heard about sheepherders and sheep and stuff like that.

Shit, maybe the guy was serious.

"Pass the coffee, would you, please?"

There were some things, he decided, that he would just as soon *not* put to the test, thank you.

Chapter 9

After six days Paula was commencing to look as desirable as one of those Paris courtesans that the history books always raved about, something that generally struck Longarm as kind of funny because the fancy history writers got all excited about the glamorous French professionals, but sneered at plain old American whores.

After six boring days of walking in sheep shit and being without female companionship—well, without any female company of the sort that would do a fellow any good—Longarm would have damn sure welcomed a courtesan or a whore or just about any willing woman and never mind what she looked like.

Of course, he wasn't really worrying. Paolo's offer of a young ewe wasn't sounding good to him. Yet.

He was, however, feeling so horny he could honk.

And Paula knew it. Damn girl not only knew it, she was having fun with it. He was sure of that.

Come evening, every evening, she'd bathe. Right there in camp. In front of him. Where he couldn't have failed to see if he'd blindfolded himself. Which he did not do to begin with.

Lordy, but she was getting better and better looking, and she had to know that she was.

The baths, in particular, were frustrating.

Not that she showed herself. That would have been easier to bear, he thought, than the way she did it. Paula's baths were an exercise in teasing and titillation, and they had him close to foaming at the mouth each and every night.

What she'd do would be to fill a bucket with water, then disappear inside the sheep wagon for a spell. When she came out she'd be wearing a man's shirt. Probably not her father's Longarm decided, because Paolo wasn't much bigger than she was, while these bath-time shirts covered her down to her knees.

She didn't wear anything under the shirt. Longarm knew that for a certain-sure fact. He couldn't see anything. Exactly. But he could, well, see. Sort of.

She'd stand right there in the firelight and take a soapy cloth to scrub with, and then a wet one to rinse with, and she'd reach inside that shirt and bathe herself.

It was hell.

The firelight shining through the thin cotton material of the shirt made it all too easy to see her figure in silhouette, and the water from the bathing made the cloth cling to her like another layer of skin so he could see that too.

And her legs. The damn girl had fine legs. Lean but shapely. And she didn't even try to hide those. She was bare-legged from mid-thigh on down, and she didn't care a lick if Longarm got an eyeful. Which he damn sure did.

By the end of each of her performances every night, he'd have a hard-on that could've passed for a marble statue if they made marble statues of such things, and it was a pure wonder that the buttons didn't pop off his fly and go zinging through the camp like pistol bullets due to all the strain they were under.

And the girl knew.

She had to know.

And her damn father wasn't any better. He'd sit there grinning and shaking his head and having himself one helluva laugh at Longarm's expense.

Then afterward Longarm would have to crawl under the damn sheep wagon with only the old dog Queenie for company.

Frustrating? He reckoned that it was. And dammit, United States Deputy Marshal Custis Long was not *used* to this shit.

It had been . . . he couldn't remember the last time he was this horny. When he was eleven or twelve maybe? If not, then pretty close to it.

No, sir, this wasn't fun at all. He wished it would soon end.

Then, dammit, the boredom and the frustration did end. And he wished to hell that it hadn't.

Chapter 10

There were three of them. Tall men on leggy, well-fed horses. They didn't bother exerting themselves, but waited in the shade of a cottonwood motte for the sheep to come to them.

Longarm saw them a good half hour before the leaders of the flock came level with the men, and even then the riders simply sat in the comfort of the shade and waited.

Paolo was walking beside the flock at the time, while Paula drove the wagon and Longarm walked close by, swinging a bit of dried wood that he'd found.

The men rode out into the glare of the late morning sunlight when Paolo reached them. They approached him, their horses looming tall above the dark little man.

Paula clucked Ichabod into a trot and sent the wagon rattling and clattering over the prairie grass toward her father. Longarm had to hurry to catch up and yank the lazy-board out from its pocket beneath the bed of the wagon. He hopped up onto it to hitch a ride, and had to cling to the side of the wagon box with both hands to keep from being bounced off the flimsy perch.

The four men, Paolo and the three strangers, stopped talking when Paula arrived with the wagon.

Longarm didn't blame them. The strangers, that is. Paula wasn't such a bad-looking girl, and any sensible man would take a moment to look her over.

Longarm hopped down off the lazy-board and tossed his piece of wood into the possum with the rest of the firewood. He thought about going over into the trees to collect more fallen wood. It was the sort of thing a camp helper should do.

But dammit, he wanted to keep an ear open here. The wood could wait until later.

The men on horseback were in their thirties, he would've guessed, and were dressed for hard work. That did not make Longarm think they were cowhands out searching for strays. Not a one of them was wearing—or so far as he could see, even carrying—gloves. And Longarm doubted he'd ever come across a working cowhand who didn't have sense enough to protect his hands from the burn of a rope. Not up here in the north, where the men threw long ropes made of hemp and dallied the free ends. A man could get away with working without gloves in the brush thickets down Texas way, where catch ropes were made of braided leather and tied fast to the saddlehorn. But not here. Here in the big, open grass country, a man needed a long rope and gloves or he would cut his hands to ribbons.

And not a one of these boys seemed to own any gloves.

They owned some firepower, though. Two of them wore two guns apiece, but not as a show-off deal strapped on as if both hands were to be used. These boys were serious about twinning their firepower, a primary revolver worn on the thigh and a second one in a cross-draw rig. Handy, that. Run out of beans in one cylinder and all you had to do to keep on firing was drop that gun and snatch out the next.

No, these boys weren't show-offs. They just figured they might want to shoot a whole lot of something. Or somebodies.

Outlaws? Longarm wondered. Could be. This route wouldn't be too awfully far off the road that linked the gold diggings at Deadwood with the railroad at Cheyenne. Stagecoaches traveling that road carried heavy strongboxes right often, and it was not entirely unknown for gentlemen with little respect for the law to want to help themselves to whatever was contained there.

He wished he knew what they'd been talking about with Paolo before the wagon arrived to interrupt things.

One of the men, a dark-haired fellow with a ferocious sweep of mustache and several days' growth of new beard, leaned over and whispered something to the man in the middle, who in turn passed the comment on to the third man.

Joking about Paula, Longarm guessed. Hell, he couldn't blame them for that. And they hadn't been rude enough to say anything out loud.

Well, if they were coach robbers marking time while they waited for office hours to open, this was their lucky day. Longarm had other fish to fry right now, and there was no need for them ever to know that they'd confronted a deputy marshal and ridden away free and clear.

Longarm glanced up at Paula, who looked more than a little nervous. He lighted a cheroot and wondered if it would help if he were to climb up into the wagon beside her. Just as a reassurance, like.

Before he had time to decide if that might be helpful or otherwise, the man who seemed to be the leader of the trio stepped down off his horse—without an invitation, Longarm noted—and stepped up onto one of the spokes of the nigh front wheel on the wagon.

The man grinned. And very deliberately reached over to lay a hand high on Paula's leg.

Longarm could hardly believe it. Cheeky? That was about as crude as a son of a bitch could get.

Longarm was standing on the opposite side of the wagon and couldn't reach the piece of shit, but that didn't mean he couldn't do anything about it.

He gave Ichabod a quick whack on the rump, and the startled mule jumped a couple steps forward.

That caused the wheel to roll, twisting the man's ankle and dumping him off the spoke. He had a clear choice. He could either jump aside or take a fall. He leaped down and came charging around the back of the wagon at Longarm.

That was just fine by Longarm, who cocked his fists and waited for the ignoramus to arrive.

Chapter 11

There were three of them, and by God it took them all to get the job done.

By the time they did, the first one, the one who'd laid his hand onto Paula, was bloodied and reeling. He'd been alone at the start of this dance, and taken the worst of what Longarm had had to pass around for all of them to enjoy.

The others hadn't been slow to step in beside their pal, and at that they might not have been able to come out on top, except the one with the mustache had enough presence of mind to stay mounted and ride his horse into Longarm from behind while the other two were holding his attention by making targets of themselves for Longarm's punches.

Once Longarm was off his feet, Mustache leaped off the horse to join the others, and amongst them they were able to swarm him under.

Even at that they were all three running blood, and would show some bruises for the next week or better.

Not that Longarm was unscathed himself. The good thing was that he couldn't feel all the hurts. Yet. That would come eventually. And hell, he could accept that.

What he had difficulty accepting was what the three did once they had him down.

42

The sons of bitches hauled out manacles and handcuffed him.

Even more amazing, one of the bastards very loudly announced, "You are under arrest, mister."

"What the hell . . . ?"

"You're charged with assault on a peace officer."

"What the fuck are you talking about?" Longarm demanded.

"You've assaulted three duly sworn deputies, and we are charging you with the crime. That's what I am talking about."

"You?"

"Me," the leader concurred. "You jumped me. Also Tim there. Also Henry. And if our testimony isn't enough to put you in a cell for the next couple months, we'll call in these good folks here. I'm sure they would testify to the truth. Which is that you first knocked me down and then offered to fight with me."

"Yes, and I'd do it again too, damn you. Do it a damn sight better, in fact, if you was man enough to stand up t' me alone," Longarm challenged.

"Nothing personal in this, mister. I'm just doing my duty. Now get on your feet. We got to take you in to stand before the judge."

"Take me in? Look, I don't know who you are, but—"

"Donnington is my name. Deputy Sheriff Roger Donnington. That one over there is Henry Adair. The deputy with the mustache is Tim Burch. Is that what you wanted to know?"

"You're making a mistake here. I . . . ."

"You wouldn't believe how many times I've heard that one, mister. We aren't the ones making the mistake. You already did that when you assaulted a peace officer."

"Look, I'm not gonna debate the facts with you. You and me both know exactly what I done and exactly why I done it. And why I still say I'd not only do it again, I'd twist your tail into knots any time it's just the two of us. The point is, now you're interfering with a peace officer acting in the line of duty."

43

"Am I now?" Donnington said, sarcasm thick in his voice.

"I'm a United States deputy marshal. My name is Custis Long, and I—"

"Sure you are, mister. You're a U.S. deputy and I'm the Prince of Wales."

"Hey, Roger. If you get to be a prince, does that mean I can be the king?"

"No, asshole, but I might let you be the queen."

"Quit funning around, both of you. The sheriff is going to want us to get this fellow behind bars before he gets loose or something. Right?"

Donnington and Adair seemed reluctant, but they both nodded. Adair jerked Longarm to his feet. The damn handcuffs hurt like hell when the steel bit into his wrists.

"I'm telling you, you are making a mistake here. I'm a United States deputy marshal and I—"

"Yeah, you sure as hell look like one, all right," Donnington sneered.

"I told you, I'm working here. I'm dressed like this ... dammit, never mind why I'm dressed like this. That's none of your business. Now take these cuffs off me before I decide to charge you with interfering with an officer in the performance of his duties. And I'm talking about a federal offense here, damn you, not some dip-shit county charges."

"I'm gonna tell you the same as I tell all the other bastards just like you," Donnington said. "Tell it to the judge. Now come along, dammit. We have a long way to ride. Tim, you're the lightest of the three of us. Take him up behind your saddle."

"Let the son of a bitch walk," Burch protested. "He was walking with these stinking sheep, wasn't he?"

"We don't have time to walk him all the way back to McCollum, dammit. Now do what I tell you and put him up on your horse with you."

McCollum. That meant they'd crossed into Warren County already, McCollum being the county seat. Longarm had thought they were several days away from Warren, but then he was mighty hazy on the specifics of the geography around here.

Perfect. On top of everything else, now he'd gone and told who he was to some of Sheriff Bennett's own deputies. And it was Bennett they'd hoped to fool with this masquerade.

Longarm figured he was having just about the perfect fucking day.

And it got no better when Donnington and Adair shoved him up onto the butt of Tim Burch's horse for what turned out to be an uncomfortably long ride to McCollum, W.T.

Chapter 12

McCollum wasn't the armpit of Wyoming Territory. Mc-
Collum was a pimple in the armpit of the Territory. A nothing
little place, flat and dry and dreary, with probably not more
than three or four hundred people living there, a scattering of
hog ranches out at the east end of town, and a collection of
single-story business buildings so sun-dried and windblown
that not a one of them had its false front completely intact, at
least none that Longarm could spot during his grand entry into
McCollum society.

The place looked well on its way to becoming a ghost town,
and the people hadn't even left yet.

The lone building of any substance was the two-story courthouse that squatted gray and severe in the middle of what
passed for a town square. Town horseshoe would have been
more accurate, though, for there were only enough business
structures to surround the square on three sides. The fourth
side was left open to accumulate weeds, broken bottles, and
other trash heavy enough that the wind didn't blow it away.

Helluva town, Longarm thought rather sourly as he rode in
perched on the ass of someone else's horse with his hands
cuffed behind him and an absolutely ferocious itch in his mustache. The itch had been deviling him for the past ten miles
or more, and the only way he could have scratched it would've

been to nuzzle the back of Tim Burch's sweat-stinking shirt. Longarm wouldn't have wanted the Warren County deputy to mistake his intent, and so refrained from rubbing up against the man.

Sure as hell did itch, though.

"All right, you can get down now," Burch said as he reined to a stop at the back of the courthouse.

"With no stirrups an' my hands chained?" Longarm asked.

Burch didn't argue with him. Just reached back and pushed. Longarm slid backward off the rump of the horse, landed awkwardly but upright, and banged his nose against the horse's tail.

The coarse tail hairs kind of scratched the itch just a little, so Longarm stayed there for a second or three and scrubbed his mustache on the horse's butt.

He heard a giggle, higher-pitched than he thought any of the good deputies would've made, and turned around to see that they'd been joined by a young woman. At least Longarm supposed she would be considered a woman. Some might still count her a girl. She was young enough, and old enough, that it could go either way depending on viewpoint.

What was not in doubt in any way, shape, or form was the plain fact that woman or girl, whichever, she was one damned pretty female.

She was slim, with a dark complexion and black hair worn long and loose. She didn't look Mexican, though. Portuguese, Longarm guessed, or Italian maybe. Almighty nice looking anyway, with a pert figure, high cheekbones, and a soft clarity of skin that middle-aged rich women would have sold their souls to possess.

She had full lips, huge dark eyes, a dainty and rather patrician nose . . . and an expression when she looked at Longarm that suggested she found him somewhat less acceptable than a turd in the soup tureen.

But then, he reminded himself, the circumstances of this initial meeting did not present him in his very best light, considering that he was in manacles in the first place, and had

47

been rubbing his face on a horse's ass to boot.

No, this most definitely was not the very best day he could remember having. The girl quit snickering at the sight of the prisoner, and turned her attention to Roger Donnington. "He saw you boys ride in. He wasn't expecting"—she gestured vaguely in Longarm's direction—"whatever this is."

"We'll explain everything in a minute," Donnington said. "Tim, whyn't you run up and tell the sheriff what we got here. Henry, you take care of the horses. I'll bring the prisoner along in a minute."

Burch seemed puzzled for a moment. Then, whatever his problem, he seemed to work it out, for his frown dissolved and he grinned and nodded. "I gotcha," he said, and tossed his reins to Henry, then hustled off toward the front of the courthouse and quickly out of sight.

Adair collected all three horses, and the girl gave Longarm a hooded, suspicious look before she tossed her head snippishly—the late afternoon sunlight caught the gleam of good health in her hair and made her all the prettier when she did that—and walked away.

All in all, her opinions of him apart, Longarm would have preferred to go with her.

Instead he had to stand there while Donnington quite unnecessarily inspected the handcuffs—damn things were tight to begin with, and if he hadn't been able to get them off in the last twenty miles, he wasn't apt to do so now—before taking him by the elbow and guiding him onto the front steps of the courthouse and inside.

The sheriff's office and jail were, naturally enough, on the second floor.

Nope. This just wasn't a real good day.

Chapter 13

Sheriff Michael Bennett was a large man of that beefy and physically intimidating sort who towered over those around him and learned early in life to walk roughshod over them without much regard for the thoughts, the feelings, or the opinions of others.

He was also one of those very rare individuals for whom Longarm took an instant—and intense—dislike.

There was something about Bennett, the look in his eye or the arrogance in his posture, that immediately made Longarm's hackles rise. He could quite literally and honestly feel a prickling at the back of his neck as the hair there stood upright and the muscles in his neck and shoulders began to gorge with blood in anticipation of a fight.

Not that he expected to fight with Bennett. Not with his hands still cuffed behind his back. But he damn sure wanted to.

It was like that. One look and Longarm was wanting to hit this man square in the face.

The feeling, he suspected, was mutual.

Bennett gave the prisoner a dark and glowering glare, and Longarm could see the sheriff's hands clench and knot into fists as he sat leaning back in the chair behind his desk.

They remained like that for several long seconds, Bennett seated but ready, Longarm standing, with the deputies in the room forgotten.

Then Bennett shuddered, almost as if waking from a sleep, and leaned forward. He picked up a pen, dipped it into an inkwell, and without looking up demanded, "Name?" His voice was not one of welcome.

Longarm did not immediately respond.

"Answer the sheriff," Donnington ordered, giving Longarm's elbow a shake.

"Talkin' to me, is he?"

"Must be," Donnington said. "He already knows us." Us at that moment consisted of Donnington, Burch, and another man, presumably also a deputy since he had a badge pinned to his shirt, who Longarm hadn't seen before.

"Name," Bennett growled again.

"Long. Custis. United States deputy marshal."

"Yeah, sure. Tell that to the judge. Now what's your real name, asshole?"

"Long. Custis. United States deputy marshal."

Bennett's scowl deepened. "Put him in number four, Roger. You boys searched him already?"

"He was carrying a gun, Sheriff. Tim has it."

"All right. We'll keep him on ice till the judge is ready to see him for arraignment and a bond hearing. Burch, you can tag his gun and put it into the cabinet."

"What name should I tag it with?" Mustache asked his boss.

The sheriff gave Longarm another long, hard look, then responded, "Make it John Doe. That will do until we find out who he really is."

"My name is Custis Long, and I—"

"And you're full of shit, that's what you are," Bennett snapped. "I happen to know there *is* a U.S. deputy marshal named Long. I've heard of him too. I also know that you ain't him. Not working as some piss-ass sheepherder, you aren't. So if you won't tell me your real name, you can sit in that cell back there till I figure out who you really are. Which reminds me, Barry, you can go down and tell Leo to get some wires off. The usual list of sheriffs and town marshals. Also to the boys down in Cheyenne. And to the marshal in Denver. What's his name again?''

"Vail," Longarm injected. "William Vail. I oughta know that. He's my boss."

"Sure he is, Mr. Doe. Sure he is. Where was I, Barry? Oh. Yeah. Get the usual wires out plus to Cheyenne and Denver. See if anybody is looking for this impostor here. If he's giving out a false name, he's probably on the run from something. Send his description around. See if it rings any bells." Bennett looked Longarm up and down. Slowly. Insultingly. "Small-time shit, I'd say. This guy doesn't have balls enough to stand face-to-face with a grown man."

"Any time you want, Sheriff," Longarm returned. "Guns, knives, or fists. You and me, one on one."

Bennett ignored the offer. He nodded to Donnington. "Go ahead now, Roger. Lock him down."

"You're going to be one sad, sorry son of a bitch when you hear back from Billy Vail," Longarm predicted. "And when you do, when I'm out of here, don't you forget. You and me. One on one."

"Yeah, sure. I've heard it all before. Roger? Get him out of here before I lose control and beat the shit out of this one, will you?''

Donnington took Longarm by the elbow and steered him through a narrow doorway into the cell block, turned left, and took Longarm into the far back corner of the jail.

Cell number four, Longarm saw, had no window, no mattress, and no shit bucket. Just a steel cot, steel flooring, riveted steel ceiling, and a gracious plenty of steel bars.

Cheerfully inviting it was not.

The deputy took Longarm inside, then carefully backed out and locked the door closed before he motioned for his prisoner to turn so the handcuffs could be removed. The procedure was

entirely correct, which did not in the slightest make Longarm
like or appreciate it.

"How about my cheroots?" Longarm asked.

"If you got 'em you can smoke 'em."

"They're with my stuff back at the sheep wagon."

"Then I expect you can't smoke them, mister."

"But what about . . . ?"

Donnington was no longer bothering to listen. He'd turned
and walked away, taking the keys to Longarm's freedom along
with him.

"Damn you," Longarm roared.

Not that it did any good. Hell, it didn't even make him feel
any better.

He stood at the cell door, staring morosely in the direction
of the door into the sheriff's office, but a moment later that
was closed too and he was alone with nothing but sour
thoughts for company.

After a bit he turned and went to stretch out on the hard,
cold surface of the metal cot.

Chapter 14

As far as jolly good times went, incarceration in the Warren County jail was roughly the equal of a tooth extraction.

The food would have been sneered at by Paolo's dogs. No one ever bothered to bring him either a pillow or a mattress to soften the unyielding steel of the cot. He had no cheroots with him and no one was interested in providing any. With neither tweezers to pull with nor scissors to snip with, his mustache hairs were growing down into his mouth, a feeling that Longarm despised.

And worst of all, whenever he had to crap or even take a piss, he had to first get the attention of a deputy or of Bennett's half-wit jailer and have them fetch a bucket.

Common sense would have suggested they leave the slop bucket in an occupied cell, but no, that wasn't the way Sheriff Bennett did things. And in this jail they did whatever Sheriff Bennett liked, damn their eyes.

So each and every stinking time—quite badly stinking thanks to all the cabbage and beans that were part of the diet here—whoever brought the bucket would order Longarm into the back of the cell, open the steel door just barely far enough to slide the bucket in, and then lock up again before the prisoner was permitted to come forward and relieve himself.

It was annoying, it was humiliating, and it was unnecessary.

But then, Longarm thought, the humiliation involved was very likely the reason Bennett insisted it be done this way. Damn the son of a bitch.

Longarm gave serious consideration to pissing on the floor when that was all the relief required. But dammit, he would be the one who had to live with the result if he elected to do that. So reluctantly, he did things Bennett's way. Damn him.

"Why the hell am I still in here?" he demanded of the raggedy-assed jailer on the morning of Longarm's second full day behind bars. "I want to talk to the sheriff. I need to see one of the deputies. Damn you, look at me when I'm talking to you. Say something. You can talk, can't you?"

Longarm had yet to hear the jailer speak a single word. The fellow collected the bowl that the morning meal had been served in—there were only two meals per day, one just past dawn and the other just before dark—and shuffled away.

Meal. Sort of. Longarm wasn't able to think of it as being breakfast. Breakfast was eggs, ham, bacon, maybe some fried potatoes, stacks of flannel cakes dripping with sweet butter and sugary syrup. Breakfast was corn pone. Hominy. Canned peaches. Something, anything, with some *flavor* to it.

The morning meal here was runny, watery, totally tasteless porridge. Mostly oats, but with a few weevils cooked along with the grain to add what hint of flavor there was.

"Hey. Hey. Damn you out there, hey!" Longarm shouted. Damn jailer had forgotten to shut the door into the office when he left. Longarm figured maybe he could attract someone's attention out there.

He did. After five or six minutes of Longarm's hollering, Deputy Adair stuck his nose into the cell block. "Can't you shut up for a minute, please? We don't get any damn air circulation when this door is shut, nor any peace from you yelling when it's open."

"Well, ain't that just extra awful bad," Longarm said sarcastically. "I want to know why I haven't been let out of here. There's been more than time enough for Marshal Vail to have responded to that wire you assholes sent the other day."

"Mind your manners, bub. But just to keep you up to date on things, that wire didn't go out right off. No, don't give me that kind of look, mister. There was something wrong with the wire between here and Cheyenne. I don't know what was the matter, but they couldn't get our messages out right off. I heard somebody say they thought it'd all be fixed this morning and the operator will be able to start catching up on all the traffic that's backed up these past couple days."

"Then I want you to make sure that telegram to Marshal Vail is the first one to leave your man's key when the wire is up again. D'you hear me?"

"My oh, my, for a fella in your position you do want an awful lot, don't you?" Adair commented. Longarm noticed that he did not sound particularly impressed by Longarm's demands. "Now . . . do you need the bucket or anything?"

"I need that wire sent. I need some cigars. I need—"

No, Adair wasn't at all impressed. Without bothering to respond any further he pulled back from the door and latched it tightly shut.

No air circulation in the office, damn them? Longarm hoped the whole lousy bunch of them dissolved in their own sweat because of it.

Chapter 15

On the morning of Longarm's third day as a guest of Warren County, the jailer shuffled into the cell block, but instead of collecting Longarm's bowl and spoon—both made of wood; wouldn't want anyone trying to carve a key or a knife out of light metal, no, sir—he opened the door and motioned for Longarm to leave the cell that he had not yet come to think of as home.

"What? Are they finally gonna arraign me? Do I finally get to see the damn judge?" Longarm demanded.

The jailer didn't answer with words, merely waggled his fingers for Longarm to come and then pointed to the door going out to the sheriff's office. Longarm grunted. But went. After all, a hike all the way out of the cell block could be considered exercise.

Sheriff Michael Bennett himself, in person, was present behind his desk. Standing nearby were Deputies Roger Donnington and Tim Burch and the one who'd been called Barry—first name or last, Longarm did not know—the other day. There was no sign of Henry Adair this morning. Longarm didn't particularly miss him.

"I want to see—"

"Shut up, asshole, before I try and think up some reason to keep you here," Bennett snapped. He pulled open a desk drawer, brought out Longarm's Colt revolver, and laid it on the desk. He did not slam it down, though, Longarm noticed. An imprudent man in Bennett's frame of mind might well have slapped the gun down. Bennett did not. Obviously he knew firearms much better than common courtesy. "Telegraph message came in overnight," Bennett said, obviously not liking to have to say it. "That marshal down in Denver says you're his, all right."

Bennett stood, came around to the front of the desk, and stood eyeball to eyeball with Longarm. The man was definitely annoyed. He acted like he wanted rather badly to take a swing at the federal man who was the focus of his attention. Longarm rather hoped that Bennett would try a punch. Getting that over with might be something of a relief to both of them.

"I could still hold you on local charges. Already talked to Judge Walker about that. He says if I want to press charges of assault on a peace officer, he'll back me up on it. And since you ain't from around here, I can ask for any bond request to be denied. The judge didn't say what he'd do if I was to ask that, and I didn't come right out and ask him. But I'm betting I could keep you here at least until your trial. Three, four weeks that could be. You wouldn't be sentenced to more than time served. We both know that. But I could hold you here, call it a month including the days you've already done. You want to spend a month in my jail, asshole?"

"Fuck you, Bennett," Longarm said in a light, conversational tone.

"Yeah, that's just about the attitude I figured you'd take. Big U.S. deputy marshal like you. I thought you'd want to act the hard case. But you think about this, asshole. If I wasn't such an easygoing man, your butt would be planted on that steel bunk for the next three weeks or maybe longer. You think about that."

"Oh, I expect I will be thinking about you from time to time, Sheriff. I just hope someday I have an excuse to come back here."

"You think I'm funning you maybe, but mister, I'd like that just fine. You come back here any old time. You and me can put on a sporting demonstration if you do. You know what I'm talking about? Have us a bare-knuckle prize fight, you and me. Unless you're chickenshit yella."

Longarm considered the offer. Damned if he wasn't tempted. Scrapping in the dirt was for small dogs and little kids. But damn it right here and now if he wasn't almighty tempted.

"Another time, Bennett. For now, I got work to do. If you and your imbecile deputies haven't fucked it up for me."

Which they almost certainly had, of course. After all, Bennett's failure to act in accordance with the law before was the reason Longarm was sent up here to begin with. And the sheriff's exposure of Longarm as a federal deputy was not going to do one damn thing to help him find out who was behind the depredations on Jorge Rodrigo's flocks and sheep camps.

Longarm glared at Bennett and received its twin in return, but put his personal feelings aside for the time being. He picked up his Colt from the desk and shoved it into the hidden holster sewn into his britches, then began to look around for his hat before he realized that he didn't have one. The cheap and ugly thing he'd been wearing as part of his disguise had been lost somewhere out on the grass when he'd "resisted arrest" back there, and he'd been bareheaded when he was brought in.

"I need a way back to the sheep camp," he said, directing the comment more at Donnington and Burch than at their boss.

"Walk," Bennett said. "That's what you were doing before. My men were nice enough to let you ride when they brought you in. I'm not going to waste the county's time carrying you back out there again."

Longarm paused for what seemed a very long time, staring at Michael Bennett. There were a good many things he might have said. He swallowed them. He'd been away from Paolo and the sheep wagon more than long enough already. He certainly did not want to give Bennett any more excuses to cause trouble.

Longarm turned and got the hell out of the Warren County courthouse, out into the clean air and sunshine of freedom.

Chapter 16

Funny thing. When a man looked as rough and as broke as Longarm did in his camp-helper outfit, and when he didn't have any money in his jeans, all of that being back at the wagon, it wasn't so damned easy to hire a horse.

There was only one livery in town, and the owner of it seemed unimpressed by Longarm's claim to be a federal employee.

"Mister, I don't give a rat's tiny ass if you're the first assistant vice flunky to the president of these United States. If you haven't got cash to lay in my hand, you aren't gonna ride out of here on one of my horses."

"I can sign a voucher. The government will pay whatever your rate is. And you can verify that I'm a deputy marshal by talking to your telegrapher here in town. He took a message to the sheriff just this morning confirming who I am. He can tell you."

"He can tell me whatever he damn pleases, but I don't happen to have any such vouchers for you to sign an' I wouldn't trust one if I had a stack of them. Fact is, mister, you ain't leaving here on horseback unless you got cash money to pay the rent with." The liveryman stepped back, spat a stream of tobacco juice only a little way to the side, and took his time about assessing Longarm's appearance, looking slowly down to the scuffed and worn old boots, then back up over the disreputable jeans and the undershirt that covered his upper body in the absence of a proper coat or even so much as a shirt. "Lemme make this even plainer for you, mister. You'll pay me regular rates plus lay down enough of a deposit that I won't be out anything if you forget to bring the horse back. You do that and I'll be glad to make you the rent of something to ride. Otherwise, mister, it's you and shank's mare and you can go wherever you please."

"Thanks a lot."

"Anytime, mister. That's what I'm here for."

"Yeah, I suspected there had t' be a reason. I just didn't know what it was before now."

"You can get just as bitter and nasty as it pleases you. Won't change a thing, though."

Longarm sighed. "You're right. An' I'm sorry. I've been having what you might call a bad couple of days lately."

The liveryman spat again. "Happens like that sometimes. It surely does."

"I'll be back."

"You do that, mister. I'll be around."

Longarm walked back into the heart of McCollum—such as it was—and followed the poles and telegraph wire coming up from the south to a store across the street from Longarm's recent domicile in the courthouse. The store, which had the rather catchy name Main Street Mercantile, proved to offer a combination of services including postal and telegraphic.

Longarm introduced himself to the man behind the counter.

"Oh, yes. Heard about you, of course." He did not bother to introduce himself in return, which led Longarm to suspect that not everything the man heard had been favorable.

"I don't suppose you'd have a bank here," Longarm asked.

"Nope. No bank. Closest one would be in Cheyenne."

"Then I'd like you to cash a check for me."

"Sure you would. I got a next-door neighbor that'd like the same thing. But you see, I know that son of a bitch don't have a bank account. You I don't know from Adam's off ox."

61

"I have an account down in Denver."

"So you say. I don't suppose you got proof of that, do you?"

"Of course not."

"Uh-huh."

"You, uh, won't take my check?"

"Nope."

"You know who I am."

"Yup."

"But you still won't take my check."

"You do catch on real quick, don't you. I expect that's why you're a deputy, right? Quick on the uptake."

"Is everybody in this town so hard to get along with?" Longarm asked with a weary sigh.

The postmaster/telegrapher/storekeeper's eyes twinkled just a little. "Nope. There's some girls over on t' other side of town that are real easy to get along with. Come to think of it, maybe one of them would cash your check. It's a mite early in the day for a body to go round there, but a man could always ask."

"How about if I send a telegram. Collect. And ask my boss to wire money to me here. Could I do that?"

"You could send the wire. You could even send it collect."

"And if he wires the money to me?"

"If you're asking would I take Western Union's check, yes, I expect that I would."

"Then I would like to send a telegram, please. To Marshal William Vail. Federal Building, Colfax Ave—"

"This is collect?"

"Yes. I thought I said that."

"You asked about it. Didn't say that it's what you wanted to do. I'm just making sure."

"Thank you very much. Now where were we? Oh, yes. A wire. Collect. To Marshal Vail in Denver—"

By the time they got the wire off and Billy Vail's secretary Henry had time to respond to it, most of the day had been eaten up with obstruction and delay. By the time he had money in his pocket and a rented horse to ride out on, Longarm was a basket of raw frustration.

But dammit, he *did* manage to get it all done, and in the late afternoon he got the hell out of McCollum, W.T., pushing the hired horse as hard as he thought he dared back toward the place where he'd last seen Paolo and Paula and the sheep wagon.

Chapter 17

It was late when he left McCollum, and he was unsure of being able to find the trail in the dark, so Longarm spent an uncomfortable night on the open grass. He hadn't planned or prepared for that, and so had to settle for a cigar for supper. Not a very good cigar either. The store back in McCollum didn't stock his usual excellent cheroots. The best they had on hand was a reasonably fresh keg of halfpenny crooks. For which the storekeeper charged a full penny, damn him. Still, it was either smoke that or go without, and Longarm had gone without for quite long enough already, thank you very much. So he bought a handful of the crooks, and looked forward to being reunited with his favored cheroots come morning.

He woke before the dawn, shivering in the damp morning chill since his bedroll too was in the sheep wagon, and had another crook and a bit of water to substitute for breakfast and coffee. His mood was well along toward being shitty by the time he crawled into his rented saddle and headed south again.

That ill humor made the rest of the leap into complete shittiness an hour past dawn when he found the sheep wagon.

It was easy enough to locate, as it turned out.

Buzzards wheeling overhead pointed the way.

• • •

Longarm had seen worse in his time. Hell, as murders went, this wasn't so much. Two people and a bunch of animals shot down. Worse than that happened in Denver most any Saturday night.

But dammit anyway, Longarm growled silently to himself.

He lighted another cigar in an effort to help keep some of the stink away—the killing had been done at least two days gone, and the bodies were bloated now and past ripe—and hobbled his horse well away from the site so he wouldn't be adding new tracks to what was already there.

Paolo lay next to the ashes of his last campfire. The little man had been shot in the face from very close range. Carrion birds and mice or other nocturnal creatures had done considerable damage by now, but even so, Longarm could see dark powder burns rimming the entry wound just above the bridge of Paolo's nose. The sheepherder had been looking full in the face of whoever had killed him. Longarm might never know if Paolo understood that the murderer intended to pull the trigger.

But it was sure as hell a question Longarm would like to ask of that man if ever he got the chance.

Paolo had not been beaten, Longarm noted. The killer's intention was not to frighten or dissuade but simply to murder.

At least a hundred sheep were dead too, scattered over the grass for some hundreds of yards west of the campsite.

The dogs had been killed. Longarm could see the black-and-white bodies lying here and there among the dead sheep they must have tried to protect.

And Ichabod. The big, sometimes cantankerous mule lay dead in his traces.

Longarm thought about that. The mule had been in harness and was hitched to the wagon when it was slaughtered. That meant the killers came either very early in the day or very late.

The wagon and everything in it was burned and blackened. The stink of smoke and burnt wood was heavy on it. The half-wood, half-canvas covering had been charred and mostly consumed. The running gear was intact, of course, but the wagon body had collapsed and everything inside save for the stove and a few other metal objects was either consumed or at the very least destroyed.

Longarm walked around, grunting and grimacing and trying to find some identifiable foot- or hoofprints . . . some damn thing, anything . . . that he could take note of and identify later on.

But there was nothing. The grass here was lush and the soil beneath it hard, and even a stout horse left nothing more than a faint scrape if it left any at all.

Dime novelists with vivid imaginations, Longarm knew, were fond of an intrepid hero finding the marks of horseshoes with conveniently unique nicks or blemishes that would identify the perpetrator of this crime or that one. Longarm only wished the truth were so comfortably easy to arrive at.

On open grassland like this, it would be damned difficult to track anything less than a herd of buffalo.

Oh, a man could follow along behind a flock of sheep, say, simply by observing the swath of grass that would have been eaten down close to the roots and by looking for the carpet of sheep shit lying there like so many tens of thousands of tiny black raisins.

But to follow one man or one horse? It couldn't be done. In this country you trailed a man by figuring out where he was likely to go next and then looking for him there.

If you knew what man to look for, that is. And if you had some small idea of where he might be headed.

In this case, Longarm hadn't the least glimmer of a notion about who to look for or where.

And the truth, of course, was that by wandering around thinking about these and other irrelevancies, all he was doing was looking for an excuse to postpone the ugly task that lay before him.

He could put it off for a week of Saturdays, though, and that wouldn't get the lousy, stinking, detestable job done.

Eventually he ran out of excuses and steeled himself for what had to be done. Then, tossing the stub of his cigar into the ashes of Paolo Laxha's last campfire, Longarm climbed carefully onto the running gear of the burnt-out sheep wagon and began picking through the black, charred debris in search of Paula's corpse.

She and her father deserved a decent burial.

Retribution would be nice too. Or justice. But retribution would probably be more satisfying than cold, blind justice in this case.

Dammit.

He began prowling through what was left of the wagon, pulling and tugging and looking for whatever might remain of the girl's body there.

Chapter 18

Paolo. Ichabod. The dogs. A hundred sheep or more. All lay in plain sight, bloated and stinking. They were easier to locate than Longarm would have cared them to be.

But there was no sign of Paula.

Whoever had raided the camp had taken her away with them. Longarm could well imagine why a man—or men— might want to do that. What the hell, if you were going to murder a girl anyway, why not have a little sport with her first, right? After all, what's a little rape among friends.

The question, Longarm realized, was just how long the murderer or murderers would choose to keep Paula alive. How long would they play with her body before they put a bullet between her eyes?

Weeks, Longarm silently prayed, lifting his eyes toward the heavens.

Let the bastards think they'd gotten away free and clear. Let them believe they could use the girl indefinitely. Let them— please, please let them—keep her alive.

Until Longarm could find them. Until he could find Paula.

Please, he begged of the unknown and unknowable.

By now she'd long since been raped and likely beaten too. Longarm understood that. It was a given and not worth considering otherwise. But as hard as that would be on the girl, he was sure she would gladly trade some days of abuse for years of continued life.

And, Longarm hoped, trade the ugliness of that experience also for the identification and capture of her father's killers.

Longarm took a last look around, then walked out away from the death camp to the horse he'd rented back in Mc-Collum.

Paolo's burial would just have to wait. If there was any chance at all that Paula was still alive, Longarm had to move. Now. He did not bother to take time searching through the burned-out wagon for any food that might still be edible. That too could wait. Paula could not, no matter how slim the likelihood that she was still alive.

He gathered up the reins of the grazing horse and quickly removed its hobbles, but did not mount.

It was impossible to trail a horse over dry prairie turf?

Fine. In that case, dammit, Longarm was just going to have to do the impossible.

Chapter 19

It proved to be easy, remarkably so, for Longarm to find Paula Laxha. Unfortunately, unpleasantly easy.

Once more it was birds that showed him the way.

He'd been afoot, leading the horse and trying to discern the faint scrapes and scratches that would distinguish the passage of a shod hoof from the natural one of a buffalo or deer, when off to the right of his line of march he spotted a small copse of willows and a lone, ancient cottonwood. There were no buzzards in the air, but the area seemed unnaturally thick with the black and white and iridescent green plumage of magpies, those other carrion-eaters of the far western territories.

Longarm felt a lurch of uneasiness in his stomach when he saw the birds. He swung onto his saddle and cantered quickly to the shallow depression that provided water for the willows and the brittle and dying old tree.

He knew he'd found the right place when he saw the dog. It was the elderly bitch Queenie. He recognized her by the gray around her muzzle. The dog had followed her master, or in this case mistress, and was standing guard beside Paula's pale and tiny body.

Longarm felt a sadness he hadn't honestly expected as he dismounted and tied the horse to a clump of willow withes, then went over to the girl.

She was naked, of course. That was no surprise. Her body was bruised from the abuses she'd suffered, and her back and thighs were crusted with dried mud. She must have been thrown down and taken close by the shallow, cattail-rimmed pond that lay in the middle of this small basin.

Longarm gave the old dog an uneasy look, but the animal allowed him to kneel beside Paula's body.

Her face was lumpy, her lips puffy, and her eyes purpled and swollen closed from the blows she'd suffered. Her hair—so pretty it had been—was a tangled, matted mess, ropy with mud and sweat and clotted blood.

A bullet wound pierced the pale, scant flesh of her left breast. She'd taken two others low in the flat of her belly. Dark bruises encircled both stomach wounds although, oddly, there was no discoloration around the breast wound.

Longarm knelt beside her and, hesitant because of the presence of the dog, lightly touched Paula's cheek.

He damn near jumped out of his skin when she groaned.

"Paula? Are you . . . ?" He clamped his mouth shut. Now wouldn't that've been a stupid question. Hell, yes, she was alive. If barely. "It's me, girl. Longarm. I . . . I came back as quick as I could. I want you should know that."

She moaned again, a little louder this time.

Longarm snatched the soiled and ratty kerchief from around his neck and stood. "I'll be right back, Paula. I'm not leaving you." He knew she could not see. Even if she were awake enough to know and to comprehend what was going on around her, her eyes were swollen closed and it would not be possible for her to see through them.

He strode quickly to the pond and stopped there for a moment. There was a jumble of footprints in the soft mud at the side of the seep. Bird and mouse tracks overlay the human prints, but one footprint stood out from the others, clear and distinct and preserved as if in dried plaster.

The sole of the boot showed a toe so sharply pointed that a man could damn near thread a needle with it, and the heel was unusually small and severely undershot.

71

Most men in this country, at least most of those who spent any significant amount of time on horseback, liked the undershot heel on the theory that it was not apt to slide all the way into a stirrup bow and allow a man to get hung up if he was thrown from his horse.

Longarm happened to prefer a normal heel because it was so much more comfortable for walking. And he'd noticed that he walked a hell of a lot more than he got thrown from horses.

Still, the undershot heel was popular in this country.

A sharp-pointed toe, however, was not. Broad toes, even squared-off ones, were not only more comfortable, they were easier to make and therefore cheaper to buy.

Whoever made this print was likely to be a horseman and a bit of a dandy.

It wasn't much for Longarm to go on. But it was more than he'd known a minute earlier.

Quickly, though, he bent, sloshed his kerchief in the water, and hurried back to Paula's side, where he knelt and tenderly bathed her face.

The girl tried to speak. Lordy, it hurt him to see those cracked and broken lips try to move. How much worse must it have been for Paula.

He held the bandanna over her lips and squeezed, allowing a little cool water to dribble onto her sores. He saw the tip of her tongue creep out from between the mashed and oozing mess that had been made of her mouth. She tasted the water and strained again to speak.

"L . . . Long . . . arm."

"I'm here, Paula. I'm right beside you." He wiped her forehead and then her neck with the moist and refreshing cloth.

"They . . . it hurts."

"I know, baby. I know it hurts." He could scarcely imagine just how bad it must hurt. "I know it does, baby."

"L . . . Longarm."

"I'm here, Paula."

"I wanted . . . you to be the first. You know? I wanted . . . to give . . . that to you."

72

"I will be, Paula. That's a deal. You and me, girl. You rest up and heal. Then you and me, we'll take some time. Go down to Denver. Or San Francisco. Have you ever seen San Francisco, Paula? It's pretty. You get to feeling better, and we'll go there. We'll take the train. I know a boardinghouse . . . no, better yet, we'll go to a hotel. I have a friend that runs a hotel in San Francisco. Fine place. You'll like it. We'll have champagne and oysters sent to the room, and we'll . . . Paula? Can you hear me, Paula? Would you like to go to San Francisco with me, pretty girl? Would you . . . Paula? Paula!"

He shook her, and the old dog growled.

But there was no reaction.

"Paula. Dammit, Paula. You can't die. You haven't told me who done this to you, Paula."

He grasped her shoulder and shook her again. Her head flopped limply and without resistance from side to side.

The black-and-white dog whined, then lifted its gray muzzle toward the sky and howled out its misery.

Chapter 20

She should be buried with her father. Longarm figured she deserved at least that small measure of respect. God knows the girl had had little enough in life. He would not want to rob her of her family in death too.

He picked her up—a little nervous about the damned dog, although fortunately the animal did not object—and carried her to the horse. She weighed nothing in his arms. Usually the body of a dead person, even a small corpse, seemed unnaturally heavy. Not Paula. She'd been so tiny that even in death she was delicate, fragile.

Longarm did not want to sling her across the horse's butt like a freshly gutted deer. Instead he mounted, still holding her in his arms, and rested the battered and violated little body in his lap for the ride back to the last campsite she'd shared with Paolo.

The birds were still busy there. They would be for days, he knew, with all the sheep and dogs to gorge on. But they would not have human flesh any longer. He would damn sure see to that.

Ugly circumstance had kept him from protecting the two in life. Longarm did not intend to be denied an opportunity to give them the care and concern they deserved in death.

He laid Paula gently beside her father's body, and rummaged once more through the debris that had been their wagon. He found the steel blade of a camp spade. Most of the hickory handle was burned away, but enough remained that he could manage a grave for the Laxhas.

While he dug he was conscious of the watchful but distant presence of the old dog. She lay close to the remains of the wagon, watching Longarm's every movement but offering no objection to what he was doing, not even when he finished the grave, pulled Paolo's body to it, and tipped the little man into the hole. The dog's head came up, her ears poised and alert, when Longarm picked up Paula and laid her out beside her father in the cold, dark loam that would be her resting place throughout eternity.

Longarm arranged Paolo's limbs and Paula's to look as natural and as comfortable as was possible, pressed their eyes closed, then found a scrap of scorched canvas to lay on top of them. The material was not enough to completely cover the bodies, but at least he was able to protect their faces and upper bodies from the intrusion of dirt.

There was no logical reason to care about that, of course. Longarm knew that perfectly good and well. He covered them anyway, and felt better for having done so.

As he climbed stiffly out of the new grave, it occurred to him that he had no idea what religion the Basque people followed as a rule, or what would have given comfort to Paolo and Paula Laxha in particular.

He supposed it didn't really matter. Not now. Besides, it wasn't Longarm's worry to have to sort them out. He figured God could do that His own self without any help from the likes of Custis Long.

Longarm filled the grave, and noticed out of the corner of his eye that the old dog got to her feet while he did so. She stood trembling and fretful while he piled dirt over the site, and gathered stones and the steel cot frames from the sheep wagon to place on top of the freshly broken ground so as to discourage digging by coyotes or other scavengers.

When he was done and moved aside, the dog Queenie came forward, dropping onto her belly to crawl the last few feet to the place where her masters were buried.

It was surely only his own imagination working overtime, Longarm suspected, but he would almost have sworn that the dog knew. And that it grieved.

Longarm thought about doing the old dog a kindness and putting it out of its misery. His hand touched the butt of his Colt revolver, and twice he almost pulled the gun to dispatch the black-and-white dog. In the end, though, he did not. The animal did not deserve that. And more to the point, he just damn well did not want to have to shoot it.

There were men he would gladly, even eagerly shoot. The ones who'd raped and beaten and finally killed Paula came quite quickly to mind in that regard.

But the old dog? No. Not today, dammit.

He left the dog lying there, its gray muzzle laid on the dirt of its people's grave, and noisily—perhaps a trifle too much so, the sound having the same bold harshness as whistling in a graveyard—pawed once more through the rubble of the wagon hoping he could find something, a jar, a box, a can of anything edible so he could sustain himself on a hunt that might require an indefinite amount of time.

Finally, richer by two fire-blackened cans of sardines and one tin with its label burnt away, he mounted the rented horse and again set out for the place where he last knew for sure the murderers had been.

He rode back to the spot where Paula had died. Where the footprints still waited.

Chapter 21

There were two men who'd raped and murdered Paula Laxha. Two anyway that Longarm was sure of. There might've been a third man present, but Longarm couldn't be sure about that. Beside the water hole there was the one very clear and distinct footprint for him to commit to memory, and a whole bunch of crumbled, walked-over, mostly obscured partial prints as well.

Trying to sort them out was an uncertain proposition at best but by the time he was done, Longarm was satisfied that there had to've been at least two and at most three men involved in the murder.

Who those men were . . . that remained to be seen. Longarm damn well intended to see it, though.

And while murder itself was against no federal law, and therefore had to fall well outside a United States deputy marshal's legal jurisdiction, Longarm figured that one gob of mud could dirty more than one thing. If he could be assigned this case about sheep marauders on the pretext that the depredations were being committed—maybe—on federal-controlled Indian reservation lands, then he could damn sure assign himself the extra and added little task of looking for Paula's killers.

After all, it was all part and parcel of the same thing the way he saw it. So there was surely no harm done if his own personal impetus had more to do with the murder of a girl than it did with the slaughter of a bunch of sheep and the stopping of a war between the white settlers of eastern Wyoming Territory and the Basque sheepherders who worked in this same part of the country.

And speaking of which, it occurred to Longarm that he'd seen only a hundred or two dead sheep lying back there near Paolo's last camping place. The flock had contained several thousand, which meant that somewhere not too awfully far away there had to be one hell of a lot of untended sheep blundering around and looking for an excuse to drop over dead. Which appeared to his mind to be what a sheep did best.

Longarm hadn't much personal experience with tending sheep. In fact, his own personal knowledge was pretty much defined by what he'd seen and done on the way from Cheyenne up until now.

But he knew a little about farming, and more about livestock-raising in general, and he always kept his mind and his ears open when those around him had something to say.

What he gathered about the unpopular forms of livestock, those being goats down south and sheep up here on the northern plains, was that a goat was a four-legged animal that spent its life looking for a way to escape from wherever it was, while a sheep was a somewhat fuzzier four-legged critter that spent all its days looking for an excuse to die.

Damn sheep could think up more reasons to take sick and die than anything he ever heard of. Well, short maybe of the even more tender white leghorn peeps. Longarm's pa used to insist on raising leghorns when Longarm was a boy, and always got madder than billy hell when little Custis would screw up and let one of the miserable varmints pass along to that great hen coop in the sky. Lordy, but Longarm did hate leghorn peeps. Had nothing against eating those few that survived to fryer size, mind, but he sure as hell did hate those noisy, smelly, shit-dripping chicks.

And a sheep was near about as tender, or so he'd been given to understand. If Jorge Luis Rodrigo was going to salvage anything out of this now-untended flock, something would have to be done about it fairly soon.

Longarm pondered that.

In particular, he got to fretting about the reason he'd been brought into this situation to start with.

Jorge Rodrigo and Longarm's friend Will Hancock were both of the opinion that it wouldn't take much more provocation to set the Basques into a war of vengeance.

The other sheepherders would very likely feel that the blood of Paolo and Paula Laxha could only be washed away with liberal applications of the blood of their tormentors.

It was an attitude that Longarm could both understand and appreciate. But one he could not condone, certainly not in his official capacity, and for that matter not as an ordinary man either.

Vengeance was best digested by any society when it was poured out from the ladle of justice.

And vigilante justice damned seldom knew when to holler whoa. A war, once started, was mighty hard to bring under the control of common sense or sweet reason.

Longarm figured it was up to him now both to do the job he'd been sent here for, and to see to the serving of justice on behalf of the Laxha clan as well.

He thought about that long and hard while he had a long drink of water and ate one of his two cans of sardines, that meal doing double duty for him by being his breakfast and his dinner at one and the same time.

Then he rose, dusted off the seat of his britches, and headed purposefully back to the horse.

He knew what he had to do next. And it wasn't a lie. Exactly. It was more like an abbreviation of the truth.

After that . . . after that, dammit, he had him a date he was anxious to keep. He intended to find the men who'd murdered Paolo and Paula Laxha and speak to them about what behaviors were considered to be acceptable and which ones plainly were not.

Chapter 22

Northeast was the direction he last knew Paula's murderers to have taken, and northeast was the direction Longarm chose now. He did not rush. There would have been no point to that. The murderers were long gone from this stretch of grass, and Longarm knew he had no chance to catch up with them until they stopped somewhere.

The thing that was in his favor was that they *would* stop somewhere. They had to. Whoever and whatever they were, they lived in this part of the country. They had homes here, jobs, friends.

They would be here. Longarm's job now was to find them. And in the meantime to stave off the likelihood of a war between the Basques and the cattlemen, who for years had counted on being the economic and political rulers of the open grasslands.

Longarm could not say with any degree of either certainty or honesty that it was the cattle interests who were behind the sheep depredations and/or these recent murders. But he could surely count on them to be blamed if things did blow up and the Basques took up arms.

He rode northeast at a horse-saving, ground-covering road jog until he found what he'd been expecting to see: a long string of spindly and none-too-tall cedar posts that were the telegraph wire linking Cheyenne with Deadwood and the Black Hills country.

If he'd been carrying his usual gear—and if it hadn't burned up with all the rest of his things back at the sheep wagon—Longarm would have been able to shinny up a likely-looking pole and tap into the wire with the telegraph key he generally carried in his carpetbag.

Both the bag and key, however, remained safe and secure in his boardinghouse room back in Denver, so this time he had to settle for reining his horse alongside the wire and jogging on to the next station.

Howards. Longarm had never heard of it, but a crudely painted sign on the outskirts—such as they were—proclaimed the name. Not Howard's but Howards. No apostrophe to show it might've been named for some fella named Howard. Longarm wondered about that, whether it was like Pikes Peak, which had slowly evolved by way of common usage and a little laziness when writing from Pikes Peak, honoring the man who'd first mapped its presence, or if Howards was and always had been properly written as he now saw it.

Either way, it was far from clear if Howards was going to survive to become a town or if it would fade away as time and travel passed it by.

Right now there were not more than two dozen structures squatting along the bank of some creek or other. There wasn't water enough in the creek to worry about finding places to ford it, so that wouldn't have been cause for planting a community here, and the only juncture of note was between a road that ran more or less east and west and the telegraph line that ran more or less southwest to northeast.

Still, for whatever reason, folks had chosen to locate here and build their houses and a handful of businesses.

One of those businesses, Longarm saw, had a drop line running off the main telegraph wire. That was where he would find a telegrapher and some contact with the rest of the world.

He reined his horse around to the front of the building—it turned out to house not the mercantile he might have expected but a barbershop—and dismounted there.

Chapter 23

The only man in the shop when Longarm entered was a lean, graying fellow of fifty or thereabouts who was sitting in his own barber chair with a book open in his lap and a pair of Ben Franklin spectacles perched on the tip end of his nose.

"You'd be the telegraph operator, sir?" Longarm asked.

"Ayuh," the man said, peering over the top rim of his half-glasses. "Also the barber, barber surgeon, and as close as we got around here to a real doctor. Also do the embalming for those that want to be shipped back to wherever home was. And I'm a pretty fair hand as a horse doctor too if I do say so. It's my skills as a highly experienced telegrapher that you'd be wanting today, sir?"

Longarm smiled. "Yes, sir." He felt of his face, which hadn't been relieved of whiskers since he had left Denver. What had been stubble to begin with was now well along toward growing out to beard length and was commencing to itch. And anyway, he was no longer playing at being a sheep-camp helper. He could make himself presentable again if he chose. "Yes, sir, I'd like to send a wire and then get a shave while I'm waiting for an answer. I, uh, don't suppose you'd offer baths in with all that other stuff, would you?"

"If you have the dime, sir, I have the tub. No hot water, mind, but you're welcome to draw all you like from my well."

"A dime, you say?"

"Twenty-five cents if I carry the water. Dime if you bring it in yourself."

Longarm thought about the temperature of freshly drawn well water in this country and shivered. The prospect of feeling clean again, though . . . "Can I draw the water now and let it set while we take care of the other things I need done?"

The barber/embalmer/whatever else nodded and smiled. "Well's out back. Bucket beside it. Tub's in that back room there. Just take the door outside to find the well. Let me know when you're done." The fellow gave Longarm a mildly skeptical looking-over, but was polite enough not to ask the obvious question as to whether someone who looked this disreputable would have the wherewithal to pay for the required services. Longarm thought that was mighty good of him, especially since none of it could be taken back once the service was rendered.

"I thank you, sir. Be back in a few minutes."

The bath did more to refresh Longarm, in body and in spirit alike, than twelve hours of sleep could have done. He felt immeasurably better once he was clean, and enjoyed his shave and a trim of hair and—hallelujah—mustache almost as much, luxuriating in the feel and the scents and the warmth of a steamed towel to wilt his whiskers. It was all perfectly grand, and the timing could not have been better. The barber, who said his name was John, was just using his smallest scissors to snip inside Longarm's ears when the telegraph key began to clatter.

"That might be the answer you're looking for," John said. "I'm done here anyway. You can wipe yourself off." He handed Longarm an only slightly used towel, used a cleaner one to dry his own hands, and went over to a desk at the side of the shop to sit in front of his key and respond to the call letters for his substation.

Longarm wiped his neck and ears, then stood, feeling physically better than he had in days, ever since the Warren County deputies had come and carted him off to jail to start this unpleasant string of events. Dammit, if he'd still been with the wagon . . . But there was no point in fretting about that. Not now there wasn't.

He idled in the front of the shop, pretending to look at a dog-eared and months-out-of-date copy of the *Rocky Mountain News* while he eavesdropped on the message that was coming in.

It was indeed an answer to his wire earlier.

COMING STOP ARRIVE HOWARDS TWO DAYS STOP WAIT
STOP SIGNED HANCOCK

Longarm grunted, fully aware of the message and fully satisfied with it before John ever finished writing it down on his message pad.

Will would be here in two days' time. Good.

Longarm went through the formalities of accepting the message form and reading it, then thanked John and paid the man for the assortment of services that he'd received.

In all cases, Longarm thought, the money had been mighty well spent.

Longarm tried to touch the brim of his hat, only to be reminded when he did so that he wasn't wearing one. His own fine Stetson was some hundreds of miles away at the moment, and even the ugly old Kossuth had been lost. Paolo likely would have picked it up and kept it for him after Longarm was taken away by the deputies, but if so, the hat had burned up with all the other things in the wagon.

What Longarm needed right now were first a good meal, then a clean shirt and hat, and finally some blankets and food to carry with him when he rode out of Howards.

Those things . . . and information. Oh, yes, he was very much interested in a little information if he could find something that would be helpful. And he certainly intended to try.

Chapter 24

Longarm stacked his selections onto the counter. The store dealt mostly in hardware, harness, and such, but it had a small selection of clothing and dry goods on one side. Longarm had found only one hat that would fit him, an absolutely huge monstrosity with a brim like an umbrella and a Montana peak crown that was taller than a good many treetops he'd seen. Everything else in the store's stock, though, was too small.

He'd taken the black hat, of course, plus two shirts, some socks, a decent red bandanna, a canvas bedroll and pair of blankets to fill it, also a small pot and spoon to serve as his camp kit for the duration.

"I didn't see any cigars," he commented to the storekeeper.

"Nope. Don't carry any. Bernie Neuwirth over at the saloon should have some."

"Canned goods?"

"Next door."

"That about does me here then. Except for some information."

"I try not to know too much, mister. If you know what I mean."

Longarm's appearance was definitely working against him, he realized. Not that he could blame anyone. He didn't look like a deputy marshal. Hell, he hadn't been supposed to; that

86

was the whole idea. Now he regretted that decision. Longarm thought it over and told the man who he was. "I'll make the question official if you like."

"You say you're a marshal. I'd expect you could show me a badge, that being the case," the storekeeper said.

"I had one. My things got burned up in a fire a couple days back."

"Convenient."

"No, annoying."

The storekeeper shrugged.

"I still have questions."

"Ask anything you want, mister. Just don't expect me to answer."

"I'm looking for some murderers. Two, maybe three of them. They may've come through here. They killed a sheepman down south of here, and . . ."

Shit! That had been the wrong thing to say. The word "sheepman" wasn't more than past the tip of Longarm's tongue when he saw the storekeeper's expression harden. The damage was done now, though. There was no taking back what was already said.

"They murdered a girl too, friend. Violated her and killed her."

"Fucking sheepherder's kid?" the storekeeper asked.

"That's right. A sheepman's daughter. Does that make her less than human?"

The storekeeper nodded. "Uh-huh. To my mind I expect that it does. I just hope they made the sheepherder watch his nit get hers before they put him out of his misery."

"Mister, the milk of human kindness doesn't run real strong in your veins, does it," Longarm declared.

"Not for no fucking sheepherders it doesn't. You owe me twenty dollars for that lot. Pay up and leave. Or just leave the stuff there and go, I don't much care which."

"Twenty seems an awful lot for these things."

"Then don't buy them. It makes no difference to me."

87

Longarm frowned. But he reached into his jeans and dragged out a twenty-dollar double eagle. He was going to have to send for more cash the next chance he got if he kept on spending at this rate.

Nice folks in Howards, he reflected. He wondered if the telegrapher would have been so friendly if he'd known about the Laxhas . . . and about what they did for a living up until the point when they were no longer living.

Damn all prejudice anyway. Longarm despised it. Didn't much understand it either. He figured everybody ought to have a chance to prove himself. Hate the son of a bitch when he presented a reason for it, fine, but not just in general. Hate was something that ought to be real particular in nature and not just spread around willy-nilly.

"Thanks," Longarm said, the sarcasm thick in his voice. "I'll tell everyone what a big help you've been."

"Fuck you," the storekeeper responded.

"An' the cheery same t' you, neighbor." Longarm touched the brim of his new hat—bumped the hell out of it actually because it stuck out in front of his face a good two inches further than his own old Stetson—and carried his things away.

The air smelled considerably better, he thought, once he was out of that particular store.

Chapter 25

"You just come from Jesse's place, haven't you?" the bartender at the saloon said by way of a greeting.

"How'd you know that?"

The barman grinned. "There can't be but one hat like that, mister. It came packed in with a bunch of other stuff, and Jesse's been trying to get rid of it ever since. Tell me something. Did he make you pay for it? Or did he pay you to take it off his hands?"

Longarm grinned. "If you have to know, it was the only one he had in the store that fit me."

"Yeah, that's about the only excuse that'd make sense, all right." The bartender smiled and extended a hand. "My name's Neuwirth. Bernie Neuwirth."

"Custis Long," Longarm said, not lying in the slightest but not offering any more details either. Probably the only reason Neuwirth didn't already know who he was and what he was doing here was the fact that Longarm had walked straight from the store to the saloon. Any delay and the barkeep would have been warned to keep his mouth closed. "Jesse said you might have some cigars?" he asked hopefully.

"I got some brandy crooks back here." He must have seen the disappointment in Longarm's expression. "If you don't mind paying for something better, though, I got a box of bright-leaf cheroots.''

"Be still, my poundin' heart," Longarm declared. "Drag the good ones out and let me try one."

"Five-cent cigars, Custis, and way out here I have to sell them for seven cents if I'm to make out on them." While he was speaking, he was reaching under the counter to produce a wooden box with the words "Cuesta Rey, Tampa, Florida" heat-stamped on the lid.

"How many left in the box, Bernie?"

"Brand-new. Never been opened."

"I'll take the boxful."

"All of them?"

"Damn right all of them. I haven't seen any of those since the last time I was in New Orleans."

"They come dear."

"So does gold. That doesn't mean I don't want any."

Neuwirth smiled and nodded. "How about I throw in a drink on the house since you're buying big."

"You're a gentleman and a scholar," Longarm declared. "Rye whiskey if you have any."

"Don't be insulting. Of course I have rye whiskey. The best."

When Longarm saw the label on the whiskey bottle, he said, "I dunno, Bernie. I may've missed something lately. Must've died and gone to heaven to've found cheroots and rye whiskey like these all in the same place." He cracked open the box of cigars, gave one to Bernie, and took one for himself. A beatific smile spread over him when he tasted first the mellow smoke, and next the smooth, smooth whiskey. "No, sir, it don't get much better'n this. Mind if I ask you something, Bernie?"

"Anything at all. I'm easy."

"I noticed sign of some fellows traveling through from down south a way. They might be some boys I rode with down in Colorado. You wouldn't happen to've noticed anybody passing through the past couple days, would you? Two, maybe three men?"

"And just what for would you be wanting to find them, Custis?"

"Like I said, they might be some fellas that I knew a time back."

"Got reason to think that, do you?"

"Camp sign. You know how it is. Fella gets into the habit of doing certain things in a certain way, others who know him see that and kinda recognize the signs he leaves behind him."

"I wouldn't know about things like that," Neuwirth said, his demeanor stiff now and suspicious.

Longarm shrugged. "Prob'ly not the fellas I know anyhow. I just thought I'd ask."

Neuwirth lightened up. But not by much.

The fly beads hanging over the open doorway rattled, and both Longarm and Neuwirth turned to see who'd come in.

Both recognized the visitor.

"Deputy," the newcomer said, nodding.

"Howdy yourself, Deputy," Longarm said.

"Deputy?" Neuwirth asked.

"Don't let the stupid hat fool you, Bernie. This arrogant, pushy, mean-tempered bastard is U.S. Deputy Marshal Custis Long, otherwise known as Longarm. He thinks he is one big-ass son of a bitch. Sheriff Bennett disagrees. Mike had the asshole cooling his heels in the county jail for a couple of days. We were wondering where he got to after Mike let him out of the pokey."

Neuwirth gave Longarm a hard look, then turned back to Warren County Chief Deputy Roger Donnington. "He was asking questions, Roger. Claimed he was looking for some friends of his. Two, possibly three men riding through from the south."

"I doubt Deputy Long has any friends, Bernie. If he asked you anything else, just tell him to fuck himself." Donnington snickered. "That's what Jesse Spoto told him a couple of minutes ago."

"He said he'd been to Jesse's store. He never said anything about that." The scowl shifted toward Longarm again. "Never

91

said anything about being a deputy either. He was trying to get information out of me."

"Any reason why I shouldn't, Bernie?" Longarm asked. "D'you have anything you need t' hide?"

"Fuck you," Neuwirth said.

"Nice folks around here," Longarm observed softly.

"As a matter of fact, Deputy, they are nice folks," Donnington put in. "And we do take care of our own. We don't like strangers coming around trying to butt in on things they don't understand."

"Such as?" Longarm asked.

"Such as any-damn-thing," Donnington said.

"Is murder against the law in Warren County?" Longarm asked.

"Sure, why? You murder somebody in this county?"

"Two people were murdered recently. But I couldn't say that the crime took place in Warren County," Longarm responded. "In fact, I'm fairly sure the incident occurred on federally administered tribal lands. So don't you Warren County boys worry your empty little heads about it. Seein' as it's a federal crime an' under my jurisdiction, I reckon I'll just take care of it my own self."

For some reason that seemed to strike a nerve. Longarm could see it in the set of Donnington's shoulders and in the way the muscles bulged and clenched at the sides of his jaw. But he said nothing and offered no overt protest.

"Mind now, Bernie," Donnington said. "Don't tell this bastard anything. You do and it'll get back to Mike. And believe me, Bernie. He wouldn't like that. Not worth shit, he wouldn't."

"Interesting how you Warren County boys seem to think you need to go around threatening your own citizens," Longarm said.

"You heard what the man told you. Go fuck yourself."

Longarm considered the possibilities. Some of them would have been almighty satisfying. But not exactly productive.

And he did not want to spend any more time in Sheriff Michael Bennett's spartan cells, mostly because he did not want to do anything stupid that would delay his search for the men who'd killed Paula and her daddy.

"Thank you for that advice," he said pleasantly. He touched the brim of his hat in Neuwirth's direction, picked up his box of cheroots—damn, but he regretted now that he'd wasted a perfectly good smoke on the barkeep—and walked out, aiming straight for the door and making Donnington step aside in order for Longarm to pass.

Longarm almost hoped the county man would try to stop him and give Longarm an excuse to work off a little steam at Donnington's expense, but the man only glared and moved out of the way before Longarm walked through him.

Chapter 26

Longarm bought a supply of canned goods, ready-ground coffee, and jerked beef from a surly and uncommunicative greengrocer. Apparently Roger Donnington had stopped there before he caught up with Longarm in Bernard Neuwirth's saloon, because the grocer already knew better than to say anything to his customer. The man also charged Longarm a good three times what a reasonable rate would have been on the items that were purchased.

The more he learned about Howards, Longarm decided, the less he liked it.

"Got a café in town?" he asked of the greengrocer.

The man scowled and pointed in the direction of the west end of town.

"Thanks. You been a big help."

The man didn't answer. Longarm picked up the used and unwashed flour sack that his purchases had been dumped into, and left the store.

He took a moment to carry his new things over to where his horse was tied and arrange things on and about the saddle, then watered the animal and retied it, then ambled along the lone street of Howards until he found what looked like a house converted to business use, with a hand-lettered sign out front inviting passersby to partake of "Eats."

That sounded like a splendid idea. Longarm went inside.

It was between the normal lunch and dinner hours, and there were no other customers in the café at the time. A middle-aged woman with limp hair and a bosom that hung low enough to cover most of an overlarge belly sat with a cup of coffee at one of her own tables.

"Hello," Longarm offered.

The woman gave him a look of dark suspicion.

"I see we've already met. Sort of," he said.

She ignored him.

"I'd like something to eat, please."

"We're closed."

"The sign on the door says you're open."

"So I forgot to turn it around. I'm real sorry about that. Fact is, we're closed."

"What time will you be open?" Longarm asked.

"I dunno, mister. I'm feeling real poorly today. Might not open up again at all."

"Yeah. Sure. Thanks very much."

The woman turned her attention to the coffee cup.

There wasn't much Longarm could do about it short of beating up a fat old woman. And actually, there were others he would have preferred to put ahead of her on a list of folks he would enjoy thumping on right now.

Several came rather easily to mind.

He turned and quietly left Howards' only café.

He mounted the rented horse, and rode it upstream along the small creek that seemed to be the main justification for the town to exist—he damn sure did not intend to go downstream; he'd had quite enough shit from the people here already, thank you—and laid out a camp.

There was no hotel in the tiny community, and while there almost certainly would be one or more private houses where they normally would welcome paying guests or boarders, he kinda had a suspicion that the welcome mat would be withdrawn if he were to come knocking.

95

Longarm built a small fire of the sort that would normally be described as hat-sized. He couldn't say that now, though. The high-peaked, big-beaked sonuvabitch he'd bought from Jesse Spoto would hold fire enough to roast a half-grown ox, so he expected he'd have to rethink that term for the time being.

He boiled a little coffee in his brand-new pot, chewed on some jerky, and decided to add some suspense and excitement to the meal by sawing open the mysterious can he'd brought from the sheep wagon, the one with the label burned off.

The can turned out to contain stewed tomatoes with bits of hot pepper cooked along with them. It wasn't bad, and went with the coffee and jerky just fine, Longarm thought.

Afterward he gave thought to his next step. Didn't have to worry about it much really. After the results he'd gotten already, damn near anything could be considered a success.

When he was done eating he doused his fire, made sure the horse was tied where it couldn't put a foot over the rope and get into a storm, then settled his spanking-new ridiculous-looking hat and headed back in the direction of damn Howards.

They might not like him there very much, but he by God wasn't done with them quite yet.

Chapter 27

"Rye whiskey," Longarm said.

The bartender, a new man, not the saloon's owner, Neuwirth, shook his head. "All out." And he did not add the normally obligatory "sorry" to apologize for the lack.

Obviously, this fellow had been forewarned not to extend any courtesies to the federal deputy. It was all right, though, to take his money. "You want the bar whiskey?" he asked.

"That's a bottle of rye on the shelf right over there. I can see it."

"It isn't rye."

"The hell it isn't. I had a glass of it this afternoon."

"I'm telling you it isn't rye. D'you want the bar whiskey?"

"Fine. That isn't rye in the bottle over there with the label on it that says it's rye. Fine. I understand that it isn't what I thought it was. But I'd like a glass of whatever is in that bottle right there."

The bartender motioned for Warren County Deputy Roger Donnington to join them. "It ain't my bottle to pour from."

"Then what's it doing back there?" Longarm demanded.

"Private stock, mister. Roger here bought that bottle just a little while ago. Didn't you, Roger?"

Donnington quite obviously had no idea what in hell they were talking about. "That's right, Ken. Just a little while ago."

"So d'you want the bar whiskey or don't you?"

This was their home field. They would set the rules. It was up to Longarm to decide if he wanted to play or not, but that was about as far as his choices went. He shook his head. "No, thanks. Seems I ain't as thirsty as I thought I was."

"Want a drink from your private stock, Roger?"

"Maybe later."

"Anything else you want, mister?"

"No, thanks." It was just a damned good thing he'd bought the cheroots when he had the chance, Longarm realized. And he *still* resented having given one to that nincompoop Neuwirth.

Longarm touched the brim of his hat to Donnington—he was getting good at finding it now, was getting used to the idea of having to reach out just about as far as his arm would extend in order to find the front end of the hat; he was pretty sure he'd seen surrey tops that covered less territory and gave less shade than this hat did—and stepped outside.

It was coming dark by now, and about the only lights he could see anywhere around were in Neuwirth's saloon or at the windows of private houses. People he could question, even surly and uncommunicative ones, were becoming kinda thin on the ground.

A thin and distant sound of merriment reached him on the evening air from somewhere not too awfully far away, and he lifted his chin and studied on where the noise might be coming from.

South, he thought. Somewhere out of sight of the rest of the community, down along the same creek Longarm had camped by, but to the south or downstream side of town.

Longarm lighted a cheroot and took a moment to enjoy the flavor, then followed the tinkle of a badly tuned but vigorously pounded piano until he found the source of all the fun.

Howards, it seemed, had itself a whorehouse. Not a grand one perhaps, but the purpose of the outfit was made plain enough by the presence of a pair of bright-red railroad lanterns hanging on either side of the front door. Seeing as there wasn't a railroad within seventy-five or a hundred miles of the place, Longarm figured they weren't there by happenstance.

The place itself wasn't much. It looked like it might have started out several decades back as a sod house or maybe a trading post, back when this country was mostly given over to roaming bands of Indians and the idea of settlement was just beginning to catch on.

Since those days the original building had been added on to in a rambling, haphazard way, so that now there was a room here and an addition there, the wall materials and roof heights and other external features varying with the whim of whoever had chosen to add each new chunk. Put all those assorted pieces together, though, and the whorehouse was probably the biggest building in Howards, and for that matter, likely as not would be the biggest in this end of Warren County.

A dozen or more horses were tied at rails down close to the creek, and several wagons were parked close by, most of them left with the teams still hitched indicating that the owners of the rigs intended short-time stays and not overnight.

Fun and good times in the old town tonight, Longarm thought as he reached the front door and tapped on it.

Chapter 28

The woman who came to the door looked first at Longarm, then down at the hat he was holding politely before him. She began to laugh. "God, mister, I love that hat."

With a grin and a wink Longarm tried it on for her, posing, turning his head first this way and then that. "You really like it, huh?"

"It's you, mister. It's really you."

"Look, you don't have to laugh quite *that* hard when you say that," he said, still smiling.

"Come on inside, honey. You can hang the hat over there. I think you're safe enough. Nobody's gonna mistake it for his and carry it off by accident." She chuckled. "Of course somebody might get jealous and steal it. If you're real lucky, that is."

"Let me introduce myself," Longarm said.

"Hell, honey, there's no need for that. I already know who you are. Been warned I'm not to have anything to do with you."

"Then I expect I'd best leave."

"Why would you do a thing like that, honey?"

"But you said . . ."

The woman cocked her head and peered up at him—she had quite a distance of "up" to look as she herself probably came in several inches shy of five feet—and said, "Honey, I told you I'd been warned. I didn't say anything about being scared. Of those dumb bastards? Not hardly." She gave him a gleefully impish look. "What are they gonna do, kick me out of here? Not damn likely, sweetheart. My place is the only source of pussy between McCollum and Fort Robinson. All I'd have to do is tell all my regulars that they're leaning on me, and there wouldn't be a county official reelected to another term. Not one. And you better believe they know it too. No, sweetie, Cora Adams doesn't have to be afraid of any man. In particular, I know better than to worry about those assholes over in McCollum."

Longarm's mouth dropped open. "Cora Adams? I . . . Jesus!" he blurted out.

The woman blinked. "You know me, honey?"

"I . . . you used to sing. I saw you once . . . it was in Pittsburgh. Just after the war. You were the most beautiful thing I ever laid eyes on."

He meant that too. Cora Adams. He wouldn't ever forget the way she'd looked that night. It came flooding back now, and he smiled and said, "You were wearing a blue gown that was cut so low in the bodice that I could see the tops of your breasts, and you had on a cameo on a wide black ribbon tied real tight at your throat. I thought . . . I thought that was the sexiest thing—I thought *you* were the sexiest thing I'd ever seen. And you were. I spent that whole show sitting in my chair. Didn't even jump up to clap or shout. I couldn't. I had a hard-on every second you were on that stage."

Cora Adams laughed with delight, and this time it was her turn to clap her hands. "I love that story, honey. Thank you. And you tell it so nice it could almost be true."

"Almost nothing. It is true. I looked up at you up on that stage, and I pure fell in love. Or into some serious lust even if it wasn't quite love. I went back the next night to see you again, but there was some redhead with no tits and no voice."

"Pittsburgh, huh?" Cora shrugged. "I played there a lot in those days. In and out. Up and down the road. Up and down

101

the river. Do you remember the name of the theater?"

"The Godfrey, I think it was."

"Sure, I remember that one. Cheap dump that one was backstage. Well, they nearly all were. And the manager. He knew how hard up girls were for the bookings. Part of the deal was that he had to get a blow job from every girl in the troupe at least once before the booking ended."

"I'd've given my left nut for a blow job from you back then, Cora."

"You can have one a lot cheaper than that now, honey." She looked at him again. "I've been mostly retired from the business since I got prosperous enough here to take on a full crew of working girls, but you're one handsome son of a bitch. I'm reserving the rights to you for myself tonight."

"I, uh, I didn't come here looking for ass, Cora. I came here hoping to find someone who'll talk to me."

"Well, the only one who will go into a room with you tonight, sweetheart, is me. And I'm wanting some loving before we do any talking. Except about Pittsburgh, that is." She linked her elbow into his and tugged him forward. "Tell me again how pretty I was that night, honey. I want to hear what you remember about me from back then."

Chapter 29

Cora Adams had to be fifty at the very least. Longarm remembered her as one hell of a woman back at a time when he himself was little more than a kid. Yet even so, she remained some kind of fine to look at.

She took him back to a private part of the lively whorehouse, into a lovely and rather tastefully decorated office, and beyond it into a boudoir that was anything but the cheap and rugged sort of room used by an ordinary whore. There, even in one of the better houses, a man would normally expect to find a blanket laid over the foot of the bed to keep the customers' boots from getting mud on the sheets. In Cora Adams's very private bedroom, there was a canopied four-poster with ruffles and lace and shimmering-smooth sheets that Longarm figured pretty much had to be real silk.

He looked around the room, at the paintings on the walls and the crystal teardrops on the lamps, and he came to the conclusion that running a whorehouse was a profession that must pay a helluva lot better than carrying a badge ever would.

Probably more fun too, he concluded. Maybe he should give it some mind if he ever decided to retire.

Retiring obviously was not something Cora had in mind.

"Take your clothes off, honey." She winked at him. "I'm only doing this because I'm a public-spirited citizen, you know."

"I believe that," Longarm told her.

"Go on now. Don't be shy. Get out of those awful clothes and let me see what you got."

Cora set the example for him to follow by shucking out of her gown quicker than he would have thought humanly possible. Perhaps her stage background had something to do with it. Quick costume changes and all that. Whatever the reason, Cora Adams at whatever age had no fat on her, and fewer wrinkles than he'd have expected too.

Her tits weren't upright and proud the way they must have been when she was young, and her nipples had spread out so now they occupied almost half the available space on those tits. But her waist was still small, her ass tight, and her legs shapely.

And if there were a few wattles beginning to show under her chin, well, that wasn't what he was looking at anyway.

She had huge, gray eyes. A heart-shaped face. Blond hair gone just a little bit brassy from all the years of chemical improvement.

Her age showed mostly in her hands. And in the fact that her pussy had dried up. Without blush or apology Cora fetched a cut-glass container of some lightly perfumed slippery fluid and greased her cunt.

Then she came over to him. The top of her head reached just about to his breastbone.

"I thought I told you to get out of those clothes."

"Yeah, I was gonna do that too. Got interested in the show and was kinda sidetracked. D'you mind?"

She laughed. "Is that supposed to be a compliment, dearie?"

"It is."

"Remind me to thank you when I have more time. Right now I'm busy, sweetie." She began working on the buttons of his new shirt.

"Honey," he said. "Dearie. Sweetie. You do know my name, don't you?"

"Somebody might have told me, but I don't remember it. Do I offend you, baby?"

He felt his britches slither south. Then her hands were stroking and grasping. He forgot what the question had been.

"My goodness, dearie. This is nice. A girl doesn't see a lovely thing like this more than once or twice a year." She pulled it out, examined it more closely, and amended her statement by adding. "No, honey, make that not more than once or twice a decade." She looked up at him and laughed. "I just *knew* I was going to like you, sweetie, right from the very first time I laid eyes on you. And speaking of laying . . ."

She took him by the conveniently provided handle and gently pulled him over to the side of the big bed.

"Let me see here, babycakes. You said something about wanting a blow job. For all those years since Pittsburgh? Gracious, what a sweet thing for a gentleman to admit. Well, lovey, your patience will be rewarded. Now lie down here. That's nice. No, on your back is just fine. Let me start things, shall we? Yes. Like that. Thank you."

Longarm'd found out a long time ago that Cora could sing. Back then he hadn't known the half of her talents. The woman had a tongue and a mouth that were sweet, soft, and hot as one of those Mexican peppers. Cora could light a man's fires every bit as quick as the peppers could.

She nibbled gently at his balls, ran her tongue slowly up his torso, and licked first his left nipple until the tingling was curling his toes, then over to the right side of his chest. About the time Longarm thought his skull was going to pop right off the top of his head if she didn't soon get down to the center of things, Cora indeed got to the center of things. Or at least to Longarm's middle.

She licked, sucked, and caressed him up and down, using every square inch of her own body to titillate most every inch of his, and then wound up bent over the flagpole that his pecker had turned into, leaning close above it so that he was acutely conscious of the heat of her breath moving so softly over his swollen and responsive flesh.

Cora turned her head to wink at him again. She gave him a coquettish little smile and then very, very gently touched the tip of his prick with her tongue. It felt as if she'd touched a white-hot poker to him, and his dick jumped and bumped in response to the slight contact.

"Ready, dearie?" she teased.

Longarm croaked out a sound that was intended to be agreement, but Cora said, "No? All right, sweetie. We'll play a little more first."

She gave him the briefest of samples, parting her lips and ducking her head, the movement serving to drive the head of his cock into her mouth. The heat of it was almost unbearable.

For a moment she held herself poised there, her mouth still open so that there was only the merest hint of contact between his cock and the inside of her cheeks and her tongue. Then she clamped her lips tight around the base of his prick and sucked. Hard. Quick, crude, and so hard it hurt.

Longarm, startled, sat bolt upright on the bed. He reached for the back of Cora's head, but she pushed his hand away and shoved him flat again. She shook her head in warning, the motion giving rise to sensations so acute they were almost painful. But pleasant. Almighty pleasant.

Lordy, but this woman did know her trade.

She let the pressure subside, smiled a little, and very slowly withdrew herself from him, leaving behind a glob of spittle on the tip of his dick to show where she'd been.

"So far so good?" she asked.

"Arrgh!"

Cora accepted that as a yes. Which was what he'd intended to say to begin with.

"You wanted a blow job, sweetie, so you can finish up in my mouth. I like the taste of cum anyway. But first I want to feel that pretty thing inside me. No, don't get up. Just lie right there. Let me do this."

She raised up onto her knees and then stood on the bed, holding on to one of the canopy posts for balance and straddling his hips. She winked at him again and squatted, positioning herself over top of his cock.

The reason for the lubrication became clear now as Cora, smiling all the while, lowered herself slowly, slowly. She impaled herself on Longarm's spear. Skewered her own flesh on his.

Her eyes grew wide as she felt his meat fill her, and she wriggled her hips back and forth a bit to force him all the way inside, giving her weight to him as she did so in order to grind the jutting bone of his pelvis hard against her clitoris.

Just that quickly Cora's eyes sagged shut, and he could feel her pussy shudder and clench as she went through spasms of pleasure, one coming after another like waves stroking the seashore. She bit hard at her lower lip and, shivering, cried out aloud as the sensations overtook her.

After almost a full minute of that Cora, sweating now and trembling, collapsed onto Longarm's chest, bending so that his cock remained deep inside her body.

"That was . . . that was . . . wasn't it," she breathed after several more minutes had passed.

"Yeah," he said. "Wasn't it."

Cora lifted her head and looked closely at him. For a moment he thought she was going to kiss him, but she did not. She smiled. "That takes care of me, sweetie. Now a little something for you after all these years."

She grinned, flicked each of his nipples with the tip of her tongue, and then hopped off him, turning so she could more easily reach his prick. She cupped his balls in the gently moving fingers of one hand and braced herself with the other.

Then Cora Adams proceeded to give Longarm the finest blow job he could remember having.

It'd been damn well worth the wait, he decided moments before drifting into a catnap of satisfied exhaustion.

Chapter 30

"Thanks." Longarm leaned forward while Cora plumped a stack of pillows behind him.

"Want a cigar, babycakes?"

"Sounds nice, thanks."

She crossed the room to where his clothes had wound up, and rifled through them until she found his cheroots, then carefully trimmed one for him, and even lighted it before bringing it to him. "That's nice," she said. "Mind if I have one too?"

"Help yourself," he offered.

She did, lighting a smoke for herself and then returning to the big bed with a heavy cut-glass ashtray that she set in the middle of Longarm's belly.

"Hey, that's cold," he protested.

"Don't be such a baby. It will warm up in a minute." She puffed on her cheroot, then added, "That's a trick I learned a long time back. If you set an ashtray on yourself instead of beside you, you won't drift off to sleep and start a fire in the mattress. Lots of people die that way, you know. The bad part is that they too often take others with them when they do. I have no problem with some drunken fool killing himself, but it pisses me off when they kill somebody else too."

"What's your opinion when it comes to rape and murder?" Longarm asked.

108

"You sound like you have a reason to ask that."

"I do. It's why I came here t'night, remember."

"I thought you came just to see me, sweetie."

"That's an unexpected side benefit. I'm here looking for some men . . . two, maybe three . . . who raped and murdered a young girl south of here. They might've come through Howards."

"Do you know who they are?"

Longarm shook his head. "Not the least idea. I can't even be certain they rode this far. I know they were going in this direction the last time I was able to make out a track, but I couldn't swear they came here."

"And you don't know who they were?"

He shook his head again. "Wish I did."

Cora's expression hardened. "I wish you did too, honey. Rape is another thing that pisses me off. Real bad, it does."

"Does me too," Longarm said. "I know men get horny and all that, but that ain't an excuse for it."

Cora snorted. "You're a lawman, right?"

"Yes, I am."

"And you still think rape has something to do with sex, dearie?"

"It doesn't?"

"Sweetie, rape hasn't the first thing to do with a man wanting pussy. Believe me, I know. I've sold more pussy than most men have ever thought about. I've drained more balls, sucked more cocks, and breathed in the stink of more unwashed armpits than I can remember. I know more than a little bit about sex. And I've been raped. Twice. The first time was by a stage manager—not that one in Pittsburgh, this was down the river in Cincinnati—who I would've blown or fucked or whatever to begin with. He could have had me along with the booking. Hell, we both knew that. So it wasn't my pussy he was wanting, but a chance to exercise power over me. He wanted to hurt me and he wanted to lord it over me, and he damn sure did. He punched me—not in the face because I was going to have to be on stage for three shows that same night—and then

109

he raped me, and the expression on that son of a bitch's face while he was doing it was about the meanest thing I'd seen my whole life up until then. I've seen worse and had worse since then, but he was a real piece of work, Ray was. I was sixteen at the time and no virgin by a long shot, but he made me grow up a lot that time.

"The next man to rape me was a fella I stole money from. He'd already fucked me. Paid his money and had his fun and then he went to sleep. I'm not proud of it, mind, but the truth is that when he woke up I had my hand in his pants pocket and was about to clean him out and slip out the door. Except I wasn't so smart then, and hadn't thought to get dressed before I lifted his poke. So I hesitated before I bolted for the door, and he got to me before I could get clear. That man beat the shit out of me and then he raped me on top of it, and I can guarantee you one thing, sweetie, it wasn't sex he wanted from me right then, it was punishment. He was pissed off and he was punishing me with his dick. He knew it, so did I.

"So, no, baby, it isn't sex that a man wants when he rapes. It's something entirely different. Might be power, might be hate, might be his way of saying he's going to teach the bitch a lesson. But it isn't sex, sweetie. It sure as hell isn't sex." Cora took a drag on the cheroot, then calmed down a little and delicately tapped ash into the glass container perched on Longarm's belly.

"These men killed the girl's father too," he said. "Then they carried her off, used her however they wanted, and then they shot her. At least three times, they shot her. Which is one of the reasons I kind of think there must have been three men involved. Everybody rapes her, everybody shoots her, everybody is equally guilty so they can all feel secure that one won't rat on the other two."

"That makes sense," Cora agreed. "I wish I could help you find them. But the truth is that firstly, I haven't heard anything from any of my girls. If one of your men was to do any bragging in my place, I'd hear about it. I can promise you that. My girls are trained. They tell me anything that might ever be useful.'' She touched his shoulder. ''You didn't hear me say that, though, honey.''

''Say what?''

She nodded. ''Secondly, I don't know of any strangers coming through here in the past few days.'' She smiled. ''Another thing I hate to admit but will is that not quite every man who passes this way comes in to do business with me. I don't miss very many, but there's a few we don't get.''

''They don't have to've been strangers,'' Longarm said.

Cora raised an eyebrow.

''This girl and her father were Basques. Sheepherders.''

''Oh.'' Cora took a final puff on her cheroot—it was barely smoked down halfway—and stubbed it out in the ashtray. Longarm could feel a sharp prick of heat through the glass that was almost but not quite too hot to comfortably bear. ''Then they could have been local men,'' she agreed. ''In that case I wouldn't necessarily notice anything out of the ordinary.'' She smiled and laid her cheek lightly on Longarm's shoulder. ''But if someone from around here did do those killings, babycakes, I most likely will hear something. Rumors, hints, nothing you could take to court. But likely something.''

''If you hear anything, Cora, and I mean anything at all, you let me know about it. Doesn't have t' be evidence I could carry to court. Anything at all. You'd do that for me?''

''Promise to fuck me if I do?'' she teased. Or, hell, maybe she wasn't teasing. Maybe the woman was negotiating. Longarm wasn't prepared to offer a definitive opinion on that just yet.

''Cora, I'd be proud to fuck you any time you want.''

''Careful what you say, babycakes. I might just take you up on that.''

Longarm laughed. And hoped he hadn't gotten himself into something here. Not that it would be such a terrible position to be in. But still, a man likes to reserve the right to say no. Doesn't he?

111

"Put the word out to your girls, Cora. If they find the killers for me, I'll fuck you till your ears wiggle." He leaned over and kissed her lightly on the forehead. A man does not, after all, kiss a whore on the mouth.

And then, realizing that full well, but thinking too of how that reluctance must make a woman feel—and whores were people too, dammit—he bent further and kissed Cora on the mouth. She tasted faintly of the salty, seabreeze flavor of his own juices, and for a moment after he withdrew from her, he thought she was about to cry.

Instead she only coughed loudly into her fist, jumped off the bed, and hurriedly began to dress.

Chapter 31

The morning of Longarm's third day in Howards he was confronted in camp—there was damned little reason to go into town since no one there was interested in talking with him anyway—by a tall, lanky man with a wild tangle of hair and an Abe Lincoln demeanor. The man had an Adam's apple so prominent, and so large, that it should have been put into a barrel with the rest of that year's crop.

"If you thought you was gonna sneak up on me, you'd have to do better'n that," Longarm said.

"The day I want to sneak up on you, mister, you will find yourself thoroughly snuck up upon." The man frowned. "Snuck. Sneaked?"

"I think it oughta be sneaked."

"Yeah, but that sounds funny."

"It don't matter t' me either way. Just know that you can't do it."

"Like hell I couldn't. I just didn't want to."

"So you say."

"I'll thank you to speak respectfully to your betters, sir."

"If I ever find somebody better'n me, mayhap I'll do that too, bub."

"Huh. That's *Superintendent* bub to you, mister."

Longarm braced to attention and executed a snappy salute.

113

"Harrumph. Yes, um, that is better. Much better," the tall man said stiffly.

"Permission to speak to the superintendent, sir?"

"Speak."

"I would request, sir, with all respect due, sir, that the sir should fuck himself. Sir."

Will Hancock threw his head back and roared with laughter. "Ah, if only I could. It'd be so convenient, wouldn't it?"

Longarm grinned and grabbed his old friend in a bear hug. He had to reach up in order to do that. Will Hancock was at least four inches taller than Longarm. And probably weighed a good fifty pounds less. Longarm had often advised him to avoid sitting still in the vicinity of any medical schools he might happen upon lest the students there mistake him for a skeletal cadaver and get out their scalpels and bone saws.

Longarm glanced behind Will. "Couldn't you get any of your boys t' come with you like I asked?"

Hancock grinned and pointed past Longarm's shoulder. When Longarm turned around he damn near jumped out of his skin. Standing behind him so close he could have touched any one of them without having to lean forward were four Indians, each man wearing a dark blue woolen jacket of military cut but without any patches or regimental insignia. Each carried a Winchester repeating rifle, the military model with full-length barrel and wooden cladding to protect the cartridge tube. Each wore a bandolier slung over one shoulder with bright brass showing in every bullet loop. Each wore a cavalry-style campaign hat, although these were liberally decorated with eagle feathers, bear claws, and other adornments.

And each man had come up behind Longarm so silently, he hadn't had a clue as to their presence so close behind him that they could have lifted his scalp before he knew he wasn't alone.

"Damn it, Crooked Foot, I've told you not t' do that. Haven't I told you that?"

The Indian on the left grinned. "Lots of times you tell me that, Long Arm. You say that every time I scare shit outa you.

114

It don't do no good. I scare you next time anyway. Funny how you jump. You know?''

Longarm grinned too, and shook the swarthy tribal policeman's hand. Then he shook with the other three, men he hadn't met before, and was introduced to them too. Small Heart, Rides Fast, and John were their names.

"Thanks for coming," Longarm said, motioning for them to join him at the fire where he had coffee in the pot and enough jerky to share.

"Tell me something," Hancock asked. "You know we're happy to give whatever help we can. But why did you send for us and not Jorge? They're his sheep, after all."

"It's because o' how all them sheep got loose, Will." Longarm filled the five men in on the murders.

"I see," Hancock said almost immediately. "You're afraid if you send to Jorge for help, the word will get out to the other Basques and they'll start the very war you're trying to avoid."

Longarm nodded. "That's it in a nutshell, Will. I'm asking you and your policemen here t' take the sheep on over onto the reservation . . . that is t' say, I want you t' herd them deeper *into* the reservation. Obviously they're already on tribal land right now, else I wouldn't have jurisdiction here."

"Yes, I would say that the sheep are on our land. And the murders took place on tribal ground too. In fact, I'm fairly sure of that," Hancock said, "subject to a survey if anyone wants to go to the bother, of course." He nodded solemnly, reached into Longarm's shirt pocket, and extracted cheroots for himself and for each of us men. He only handed out three of the smokes, though, dropping the last cigar into his own shirt pocket. "Rides Fast doesn't smoke. I'll smoke this one for him later. You know. To keep from offending him."

"Ugh," Rides Fast said, keeping a perfectly straight face when he did so.

"I dunno," Longarm mused. "Maybe I shoulda sent for Rodrigo after all. He wouldn't of inflicted a bunch of damn clowns on me."

"No," Hancock agreed. "Just a bunch of blood-crazed

Basques with shotguns and sharp knives. If you think that would be an improvement . . ."

"Seriously, dammit, I'm glad you're here. Thanks. And look, when you get down there, take a look around at the campsite and out by the pond where the girl was killed. I'm a fair hand as a tracker, but I know my limitations. If any of you comes up with anything you think I oughta know, I'd be glad t' listen to whatever you have to say."

"Where will you be?"

"From here I'll go over t' McCollum again. It's the county seat. If there's any rumors floating around, maybe some of them will wind up there. For sure I'm not doing any good around here. Hell, nobody will talk to you."

"Ah," Crooked Foot said. "People here know you pretty good, eh?"

"I'll be in McCollum at least for a while," Longarm said, keeping to the serious business at hand again.

"What about dog?" Crooked Foot asked.

"The dogs were shot. All except the old mother. She stayed at the graves. If she's still there, maybe you can convince her t' go along an' help with the sheep."

"Old dog, you say. Black and white? Gray around face?" the policeman asked.

"That's right. They called her Queenie."

"She not at grave now."

"How would you know a thing like that?" Longarm asked.

"No magic," Crooked Foot said with a grin. "She sitting in those willows." He pointed. "There."

"You're full of shit."

Crooked Foot didn't argue. He took a chunk of jerky from the bag Longarm had set out, snapped off a small bite for himself, and tossed the rest of the stick over to the side of the small clearing where Longarm had set up his camp.

For a moment nothing happened. Then the willows parted. Queenie crept out just far enough to snatch up the jerky, and then darted back into the protection of hiding.

"I'll be damned," Longarm said. "I wonder how long she's been hanging around. And what for. Damn dog never liked me."

116

"Still doesn't," Crooked Foot said. "Wouldn't stay over there if she like you."

"Well, I been insulted by worse than her. But now that I know, I reckon I might as well feed her something. She must be awful hungry if she's been living on rabbits or mice or shit like that."

"Do you want us to stand by in case you need help making any arrests or anything?" Hancock asked.

"I wish to hell I had somebody to arrest, Will, but the truth is I don't have one suspect, much less the whole pack of the bastards, ready to wrap up and put in irons. No, just take care o' those sheep if you would. An' take a look to see can you figure out any more from what you see there than I was able to. That's another part of why I wanted you and your boys t' come instead of Rodrigo and his Basques. I'm blind on this one so far, Will. And I hate it. Paolo and his girl deserve better than what I'm able t' give them right now. I'm hoping maybe you can help."

"If we see anything, Longarm, we'll find you. McCollum, wherever. Otherwise we'll take the sheep on back to ... that is, we'll drive the sheep deeper into the reservation that they're already on ... and you won't hear from us again unless you send for us. Fair enough?"

"More than." Longarm stood and formally, ceremoniously shook hands with each of the men, starting with the quiet policeman named John and ending up with Agency Superintendent Will Hancock. "Thanks, boys. I truly appreciate you coming all this way just on my say-so."

"You would do the same for us. We know that."

Longarm grinned and clapped his old friend on the shoulder. "Bullshit I would. And I mean that most sincerely."

"Next time, Long Arm," Crooked Foot said, "I clip lock of your hair before I say hello."

"Bullshit," Longarm said again. But he wasn't so sure that it was. Crooked Foot and his men were damned good at what they did.

Chapter 32

The operator of the McCollum livery stable seemed near about overwhelmed with joy to see Longarm's return. The man was seated on a nail keg, using waxed, heavy thread to stitch some sort of repair to a piece of harness. When he saw Longarm—or perhaps more to the point, when he saw that the horse he owned was still alive and moving—he turned his head and spat. It was as close to a welcome as Longarm figured he would get.

"Give me a minute to finish this," the livery man said, concentrating on the bit of leather in his hands. "I'll refund your deposit when I get done here."

"Thanks, but I'm not done with the horse yet."

"You want him put up here, is it?" The fellow spat again. "I do."

"Fifty cents a day for hay and a stall. Fifteen cents more if you want him grained."

"It's your damn horse, mister. Feed him yourself."

"Yours whilst you have him rented. Your responsibility."

"I'll be damned if I'm gonna pay you rent and a board bill both at the same time," Longarm protested.

"Then stand there a minute. I'll go fetch the refund of your deposit like I said."

"Fuck you." Longarm was becoming more than a little weary of the attitudes he was encountering in Warren County, Wyoming. "You're already charging me two dollars for the rent. I'll keep on paying that whether I use the horse or not, just so I can count on it being here and ready for me if I need. But I'm not paying anything over that, and that's final."

The livery man spat, tilted his head, and peered up at Longarm for a spell, seeming to ponder the likelihood of finding another renter for the animal, and probably also wondering if Longarm meant what he said about quitting the deal if a board bill was tacked on.

The truth was that Longarm was bluffing as bad and as bald as a drunken cowboy at a convention of Baptists. Longarm figured it was entirely possible that he might need a horse in a hurry, and he intended to hang on to this one whatever it took. But the liveryman didn't have to know that, damn him.

Eventually the liveryman looked away, spat one more time, and said, "All right, damn it. But the two dollars a day keeps running."

"That's fair," Longarm said. "Just make damn sure if I want that horse he's there. Don't be giving him out to nobody else so long as I'm paying for the use of him."

"I said all right, din' I?"

Longarm grunted an acknowledgment and began to unsaddle. He hung the saddle, blanket, and bridle on the pegs where they had been when he'd first come here some days earlier, and returned the horse to the same stall. The livery man, big help that he was, remained sitting on the nail keg. Longarm rather hoped a stray nail would work its way up through the lid and stick the man in the ass.

"Is there a boardinghouse in town?" he asked when he had his few possessions in hand and was ready to go.

The liveryman gave him a sly smile. "I expect you could always find a way to get your same room back."

Lordy, sometimes it seemed that everybody in this whole county not only knew who Longarm was, they knew his local history too.

"I was thinking 'bout something with a mite softer bed than the sheriff provides for his guests."

The liveryman spat, paused for a moment as if debating whether he should offer information without a fee being attached, then pointed. "Miz Benson. Lives in the house with green shutters over that way. She's a widow woman. Takes in strangers when we got some." He grinned. "If she feels like it. She's notional, Miz Benson. She don't like the look of a man, she'll just shut the door in his face."

"Notional is a popular outlook around here," Longarm offered.

"Yeah, I've heard that said before. All in how you want to look at it. I suppose."

"I'll tell Mrs. Benson you sent me. She's sure t' be grateful."

"You do that, mister. You just do that."

Longarm picked up his bedroll. "By the way, neighbor."

"Yeah?"

"While we been talking you went an' sewed that brace onto your britches."

The liveryman looked down, cussed loudly, and tried to fling the piece of harness down in disgust. It didn't fly very far, though. One loop of the stout, waxed cording had caught in a fold at the front of his trousers.

Longarm ambled off down the street, whistling a light tune.

Chapter 33

The green door, painted to match the shutters on the house, was opened by a fat woman in her sixties or thereabouts. She had white hair and a mustache that wasn't as fine and full as Longarm's, but which was mighty luxuriant for a woman to be sporting.

Longarm was considerate. He didn't laugh at her.

Mrs. Benson was less considerate. She took one look at him and burst into loud, braying laughter. "God, mister, I love your hat."

Longarm had gotten so used to the hat that he almost forgot the spectacle it presented. "You can see by my outfit that I am a cowboy," he said in a dry, droll tone.

Mrs. Benson took that one in, and began to laugh all the louder. But this time there was friendliness in the sound of it. "I don't know who you are, mister, but you sure don't take yourself too serious."

Longarm removed the hat and held it in front of him. "I've noticed, ma'am, that nobody else does, so why should I?"

She pushed the door open. "You'll be looking for a room, of course. That's the only reason anybody comes here to see me anymore. Truth is, that's the only reason I rent out rooms. My late husband left me well provided for except for somebody to talk to. Taking in boarders gives me an ear to bend."

She looked him over as he stepped inside. "You wouldn't be interested in taking up with a rich widow, would you?"

"I might if it was just up t' me," Longarm lied, "but my wife might not be so understanding 'bout it."

"You're married?" The fat old woman faked a big sigh. "All the best ones are, they tell me. Come in. You can have the room in the back corner—no, on the other side, mister, that's right. Dollar and a half a day, but that includes all meals, and if I do say so I'm a fine cook. My late husband died a happy man, I don't mind telling you."

Longarm smiled. "You know, ma'am, I'll bet he truly did."

"Go along now. You can put your things in there. Are you hungry, mister? I'm about to start cooking supper. It wouldn't fash me none to fix you a little bite to hold body and soul together until it's ready, though. Go on. Settle yourself in the room there and then you can come join me. I'll have a snack laid on by the time you come to the kitchen."

Snack, she called it. Longarm had seen four-course meals in classy hotels that couldn't compare with Mrs. Benson's snack. He was willing to bet that the late Mr. Benson had not only died happy, the man had died fat. And likely enjoyed every mouthful of getting that way too. The woman could bake pies that a man would kill for, and she'd even whipped some fresh cream to a froth that she ladled over the top of the pies. Pies, plural. There were two kinds, peach and apple, and she gave him a wedge of each. With the whipped cream. And apologized that the cherry pie wasn't done yet but would be ready in time for supper. And this was *after* she stacked his plate with cold fried chicken, a warmed-over pork chop, and some potato pancakes that she explained he would do her a big favor to eat because they were a fine way to get rid of leftover mashed spuds.

Snack. Right.

"You haven't told me your name," she suggested along about the time Longarm got to thinking about loosening his belt a notch. Or several.

"'T' tell you the truth, ma'am, I been avoiding that. You might not want me as a boarder."

"You on the run from someone, son?"

It wasn't everyone who could get away with calling him "son," but from Mrs. Benson it sounded kind of natural and even nice. "Not that I know of, ma'am." He hesitated half a second, and then confessed to who he was.

"Oh, really! I've heard about you, of course. Everyone has."

"If you want me t' move out, ma'am . . ."

"Piffle. Don't be silly. Of course you'll stay here. I think you'll find that not everyone in McCollum cares what George Walker wants or says or does."

"George Walker?" Longarm couldn't recall hearing that name before, although he wouldn't actually have sworn to it. "I thought Sheriff Bennett was the power around here."

"Michael somebody important? Not likely. Mikey Bennett doesn't run to the outhouse to squat until George Walker tells him to."

Mikey Bennett, eh? If there were few who could call Longarm "son," then he suspected there were even fewer who would even think about calling Michael Bennett "Mikey."

Mrs. Benson was still talking. It was something she obviously liked, and just as obviously had little opportunity to do. "George is sitting as county judge right now. He used to be chairman of the board of county supervisors, but I think he liked the idea of having everyone call him Judge. Or your honor. So he had himself elected county judge. When his term of office is up, I've heard tell he might go back to running the board of supervisors . . . well, he still runs it anyway, but I mean he might take the office again himself. The rumor is that next term he's going to let Mikey be the judge so he can have folks speaking to him respectful."

"Folks aren't respectful of the sheriff now?" Longarm asked.

Mrs. Benson snorted derisively. "Not unless George Walker tells them to."

"Walker runs the whole show around here, does he?"

"Lock, stock, and barrel," Mrs. Benson agreed. "Here, let me cut you another little slice of that peach pie."

"Ma'am, I couldn't hold another bite."

"You've hardly eaten anything. Are you sure?"

"Positive," Longarm assured her.

"What was I saying? Oh, yes. About George Walker. George and his brother came here in the early times. Cattle. Cattle and horses. They raise some of the best draft horses in the country. Raise and train them. And the most cattle if not the best."

"Not the best? You were giving me the impression that this Walker fella had it all. Why wouldn't he have the best too?" Longarm asked, eyeing the remains of the peach pie. Damn but it was awful good. Maybe one more *tiny* mouthful . . .

"George could afford the best. He certainly could do that," Mrs. Benson was saying.

Longarm reached over, sliced a very small wedge of the pie, and slid it onto his plate, which garnered a hugely satisfied smile from Mrs. Benson.

"George's problem is that he's a stick-in-the-mud. Other cattlemen in the country have improved their stock by bringing in some of the English breeds. Lots of English among the ownership groups of the bigger ranches up here. I don't know if you were aware of that, but . . ."

"Yes, ma'am, I did know that."

"Exactly. And those men have been helpful about finding very fine breeding stock among their beef breeds back in the British Isles. They've brought bulls in all the way from England, Scotland, someplace called Aberdeen too."

"I think that's in Scotland, ma'am."

"Is it? I wouldn't know about that. My late husband was the one who kept up with such things. He was a cattleman too, you see. He sent off for books and took all the journals and professional bulletins. Yes, he kept up with all of that. That is why I know so much about it myself, you see."

"Yes, ma'am." Damn, but that pie was wonderful. Longarm felt as though his belly might burst wide open, but if he could've forced another mouthful down, he sure would have done it.

"My late husband had a fine breeding program going. Right up until the day he had the accident and was taken from me, the dear man. I miss him still, I·surely do."

"Yes, ma'am, I can see how you would."

"George Walker, on the other hand, is an old fuddy-duddy. What the young people would call a fogy. Don't look at me so funny. I will have you know I keep up with these things. I supervise the young people at the Methodist church here in town. I know what the youngsters call George Walker behind his back. And they're right too. He is an old fuddy-duddy. George Walker took over my late husband's grazing when my Sydney passed. The fool man let all that fine bloodstock go to waste. He insists nothing should ever change. Says the good old Texas longhorn was what built this country and by God it's the longhorn that will preserve it. The man hasn't sense enough to upgrade his livestock. He raises cattle that are slow to mature and slow to gain weight and need way more grass to range on. He has to keep his cattle longer before they're ready to take to market, and even then they don't reach the same weight or have the same quality of beef cuts as the newer breeds do. It takes him longer and it's costlier for him to raise his beeves, and then when he finally does sell them he gets a lower price for them. Do you see now why I would call him a fuddy-duddy, Marshal?"

"Yes, ma'am." He couldn't possibly hold any more pie. But one more sip of coffee would be good. He reached for the pot.

"How about one more tiny little piece of the apple? Just to keep things balanced, so to speak."

Longarm groaned. But he didn't fight the old woman when she cut another all-too-generous slice of the apple pie and deposited it on top of the crumbs that were left from his previous excursions into culinary excellence.

Chapter 34

Longarm headed out for a walk with no particular destination in mind. He figured he needed to do something to work off Mrs. Benson's snack, or else he might not be able to fully appreciate supper when she had it on the table. And wouldn't that be a disaster.

He headed for the business district with no particular plan, but with the vague notion that if he happened to bump into a tot of rye whiskey, its warmth would be considered medicinal in a belly so full he was hurting.

Unlike Howards, McCollum had a complete selection of diversions for a man to choose among. There were three saloons and two hog ranches, as far as Longarm could tell. Oh, happy day. Right!

He more or less aimed himself in the direction of the closest of the saloons, but didn't quite make it. He was still half a block away when Roger Donnington spotted him and wheeled his horse in front of Longarm to block his path.

Longarm peered up at the Warren County deputy and said, "I think I'm gonna start calling you Penny. 'Cause they say a bad penny will keep turning up. An' here you are again. Come to think of it, everywhere I go lately, there you are again. So tell me, Penny, is it trouble you're looking for? Because I'm about half of a mood to give you some."

"No trouble," Donnington said. "This time." The man's eyes narrowed, but he chose not to elaborate. Not that he needed to. Next time, perhaps. "I've been looking for you," he said. "Got a message to deliver."

"Fine. Deliver it and get outa my way," Longarm told him.

"Judge Walker would like to see you."

"And if I don't wanta see him?"

Donnington grinned. "I'd like that just fine. Sheriff Bennett says if you give me trouble I can place you under arrest. I did see you spit on the sidewalk back there, didn't I? Yeah, I'm pretty sure of it. So if you want, I'll arrest you and carry you before the judge in manacles. Again."

"There's not but one of you this time, Penny. An' I might not be inclined t' be so agreeable anyhow."

"I can take you, Long. Don't ever think that I can't. An' quit calling me Penny."

"What does this pissant judge of yours want?"

"He didn't say."

Longarm thought it over. It would give him a helluva lot of personal satisfaction to beat shit out of Roger Donnington. But it wasn't personal satisfaction that brought him here, and there was always the chance that he might learn more by talking with this all-powerful judge of theirs than he would by standing in a saloon sopping up drinks like a sponge.

"He over at the courthouse?" Longarm asked.

"Nope. Wants to see you out at his house. Take the road north out of town about two, two and a quarter miles, then the wagon track off to the west from there. You can't miss it."

Longarm worried about the sort of idiot who'd claim no one could miss this thing or that one. Longarm had known men who could miss finding their own peckers if the directions were written in the palms of their hands. Still and all . . .

"You can tell him I'll be along directly."

"Tell him your own self. I'm not the one that was invited." Donnington jerked his horse's head around, spinning the animal into Longarm in an effort to either knock Longarm down or make him back water.

Longarm didn't play the bastard's game. Instead he stepped into the horse's shoulder and grabbed its chin strap. He shoved, the bit cutting hard into the animal's mouth so that it squatted and began trying to scramble backward on its haunches.

"Goddammit," Donnington shouted as the unexpected movement very nearly unseated him there in the street for everyone to enjoy watching.

Longarm stood firm. Waiting. If Roger Donnington wanted to push it any further . . .

But he didn't. The Warren County deputy gave Longarm a venomous glare, but regained control of his horse and turned it away, walking it wide of Longarm before raking the animal with his spurs to jump into a hard run toward the south end of town.

Longarm stood watching for a moment. Then he took his time about lighting up an after-snack smoke and changed direction, this time heading not for the saloon but for the livery at the far edge of McCollum.

Judge Walker awaited.

Chapter 35

Longarm didn't miss it. He could have if he'd really put his mind to trying, he supposed, but the fact was that he didn't miss it.

And the Walker ranch would have been fairly hard to miss even if a man wanted. The headquarters was as big as any he'd ever seen, and twice as grand as most.

Apart from a huge, sprawling two-story house with chimneys at each end and a third in the middle, there were barns and outbuildings, corrals and working pens that covered at least ten acres and possibly more. The pens were filled with heavy-bodied draft horses. Mostly mares, Longarm saw as he came near, and an assortment of younger stock that he guessed would be in various stages of training.

Sheer curiosity took him past the house to peek inside the biggest of the buildings, which proved not to be a barn, but a mammoth indoor training arena where horses could be worked at any time of year and in any weather.

The yard was littered with stoutly built wagons and rugged single-axle training carts, and the payroll for this part of the operation must have been enormous. Longarm could see half a dozen men working with the leggy, barrel-bodied young draft stock, and there were undoubtedly many more hands required to work with the beef side of the outfit.

He was impressed. Genuinely so. Walker's WWW spread wasn't just big, it seemed mighty well run, regardless of Mrs. Benson's opinions about longhorn beeves and the upgrading of bloodlines.

Longarm waved away a man who'd noticed his arrival and was coming to greet him, turned his horse aside, and rode back to stop in front of the house. He tied the horse to a rail there and mounted the steps to a wide, portico-shaded porch with rocking chairs lined up along the freshly painted floor, each pair of rockers equipped with a matching table that had a chess- or checkerboard inlaid in its surface.

Longarm barely had time to admire the front door, a confection of frosted-glass panels leaded into a fleur-de-lis design, before the door was opened by a servant with coal-black skin, a cutaway coat, and no trace of smile or welcome apparent in his expression.

"I believe the judge is expecting you, suh." The butler—if that was what he was—extended a hand, palm upward. It took Longarm a few seconds to figure out that he wasn't asking for a tip; he intended to take Longarm's hat. Which he managed to do without any change of expression.

This man was, Longarm thought, about the only person he'd yet come across who didn't really admire that billiard-table-size hat.

"This way, suh."

Longarm followed. He would have liked to have a minute or two just to take in all the grandeur that Walker had provided for himself out here in the middle of the big grass. Lamps, oil paintings, Persian carpets, polished hardwoods in every direction. It was something, all right.

But then Longarm hadn't been invited here to take in the scenery. He felt reasonably sure about that.

He followed the Negro servant down a hallway and into what turned out to be a paneled den or office. In another house such a room probably would have been deemed cozy. This one was built on much too large a scale for coziness.

There, seated stiffly as if waiting without anything to talk about while they waited, were three people. Sheriff Michael Bennett, the dark-haired girl Longarm remembered seeing on the street beside the courthouse the first day he was brought into McCollum, and a gray-haired, rather distinguished-looking gentleman who was formally dressed in waistcoat, tie, and smoking jacket, velvet lapels and all.

Hizzoner the judge no doubt, Longarm told himself.

He considered clicking his heels and bowing, but rejected that notion in the rather unnerving belief that this Walker person might not understand that the gesture would be facetious.

Discarded too the idea of telling the man to fuck off. Not that Longarm objected to the rudeness of it, but it probably would keep him from learning anything of interest here.

Finally, he accepted the least interesting but likely the most productive of the choices that were available to him.

He introduced himself and waited to see what the hell was gonna come next.

Chapter 36

Walker was a tall man with puffy Burnside whiskers but no mustache, eyes the color and apparent softness of ball bearings, and a ramrod carriage that would have looked appropriate for a colonel in the army, but came off as arrogant pomposity in this old man. Longarm judged the judge to be in his late sixties or perhaps into his early seventies.

He was not at all surprised that Longarm had come to him. After all, the judge had so decreed, hadn't he?

Instead of speaking to Longarm now, though, Walker turned to the girl and said, "You may leave us now, Amanda. You will please take note of the fact that we have been joined by Deputy Marshal Custis Long. Go now, my dear."

The girl inclined her pretty head in assent, rose, and curtsied to the judge before gathering several bushels of gown and crinolines and doing as she was instructed.

Longarm noticed that Michael Bennett—Mikey, that is—stood when the girl Amanda did, but Walker remained seated as if by right of royalty. Longarm himself bowed slightly as she passed, but if she even saw, she gave no indication of it. Her eyes were straight ahead and her shoulders—pale, bare, and damned fetching in appearance—held stiff and square. Longarm gathered that her part in this obviously staged little tableau was over and done with. She'd been instructed to make note of the fact that he was here and that he was alone now in the room with the sheriff and hizzoner. For whatever that was worth.

Walker waited for the girl to depart, then motioned that Longarm would be allowed to sit in the chair the girl had just vacated.

"Would you care for something, Long? A brandy perhaps? A cigar?"

"A cigar would be nice, thank you."

"Brandy as well?"

"Just the cigar, thanks." Longarm figured any man who would build himself a house like this one would have cigars of a quality to match, and that was something Longarm wanted to taste for himself.

Walker reached down and tugged at a bell cord that seemed to be attached to the small table at his side. It was an unusual arrangement, but handy enough. Probably ran under the flooring instead of up and through the walls, Longarm reasoned.

Within seconds the black man appeared, was told to bring the cigars, and left only to return moments later wheeling a cherrywood cart. The cart held several expensive cigar cases, a silver tray that held a polished silver cigar cutter, and a tiny silver chalice containing a bunch of ordinary kitchen matches.

The butler ceremoniously removed the lids from first one case and then another, holding them for Longarm to savor the smell of each different leaf until all had been presented. Then, without speaking, he lifted an eyebrow.

They all smelled the same to Longarm. He pointed to a case in the middle. The butler lighted a candle, trimmed the twist off the end of the cigar, and carefully warmed it before presenting the stogie to Longarm and holding the candle so he could light it.

Yeah, it was all just impressive as hell. The disappointment was that the damn cigar, now that he had the thing going, didn't taste as good as Longarm's own cheroots.

Still, a man had to appreciate fine theater wherever he found it. Cora Adams would have loved all this shit.

The butler offered the cart to the others, but was waved out of the room by Walker.

"Perhaps we can come down to business now, shall we?"

"I'd be obliged," Longarm said.

"First, you do understand that whatever transpires inside the confines of this room, I have witnesses who will attest first to your presence here this evening and secondly"—he looked pointedly in the direction of Sheriff Michael Bennett—"as to whatever may . . . or may not . . . be said here."

"I kinda figured that much already," Longarm admitted.

"My man Burch tells me your reputation is such that you cannot be . . . I know of no way to put this delicately . . . that you cannot be bought."

His man Burch, huh? And all this time Longarm'd thought Deputy Tim was the sheriff's. Well, he'd been wrong about things before now. Likely would be again someday too.

"I've never claimed that I can't be bought, your honor. I've heard it said that every man has his price, so I'm not fool enough to claim I'm any different." He grinned. "But I tell you true, I won't come cheap. I never yet came across any son of a bitch rich enough t' buy me. Or desperate enough either."

"Would a thousand dollars tempt you?" Walker asked.

"Tempt me t' do what?" Longarm returned. That question lay at the heart of what he'd come here to learn, after all.

"I do not believe it would be appropriate to discuss specifics of the . . . shall we say . . . behavior required. Not until negotiations get past the point of initial contact."

"In that case, you honor, I would have t' say that a thousand dollars might convince me t' do certain things. I'd sell you my hat for that. I'd even part with my best pair o' boots for a thousand dollars. But for my name or my reputation? I'm afraid you're a far piece from even coming close to buying those."

"Two thousand then?"

Longarm chuckled. "Your honor, you really shoulda paid more attention to your man Burch. I said you wasn't close an' I meant it. But if you really want, you lay out exactly what it is that you'd be wantin' me to do . . . or wantin' me to *not* do, which I'd guess is closer to the truth o' the matter . . . and then we'll see what we can see."

"I don't like for people to refuse me, Marshal Long."

"Judge, I don't like it a hell of a lot my own self. But it happens, time to time, whether I want it to or not."

"I would like to be your friend, Marshal," Walker persisted. "I can be very generous with my friends."

"Fine. Tell me what you'd like a friend like me t' do for a friend like you. That's all I'm asking."

"Three thousand, Marshal. It is my final offer."

"Tell me what for, your honor. Might be something I wouldn't mind doin'. You never know till you ask."

"It would be . . . unwise . . . for me to say more, I believe."

"A man could make a case for this t' be unwise right to start with, your honor. Tryin' to bribe a federal officer is considered illegal in some places, y'know. Like in these United States of America, which, if I'm not mistaken, the territory o' Wyoming still is."

"Bribe, Marshal? I know nothing about any bribery attempts. Do you, Sheriff?"

"No, sir, your honor, I couldn't say that I do. Wasn't no talk about anything like that that I heard."

Longarm smiled and puffed on his cigar. Damn thing didn't come close to tasting as nice as his cheroots, now that he thought on it. In fact, there was something about this whole room that didn't taste or smell right.

He stood, dropped his cigar onto the brilliant red, gold, and navy-blue patterns in the silk of the judge's undoubtedly expensive Persian carpet, and used the toe of his boot to slowly, thoroughly grind the cigar to shreds.

"You boys have yourselves a pleasant night now, hear?" Longarm said cheerfully.

He did not wait for the butler to come see him to the door.

Chapter 37

Longarm wasn't sure what was going on here or whether it had anything to do with the death of Paula and Paolo Laxha, but one thing he was completely certain about.

Three thousand dollars was one hell of a lot of cash money. Several years' wages for a United States deputy marshal. Closer to six or seven years' income for an ordinary working stiff.

And no one, no matter how rich, was going to offer that kind of money for anything less than a very important service.

There was something happening here that George Walker and his minions—Longarm thought Mikey Bennett and the boys could reasonably be termed minions—did not want Curtis Long to know about. More specifically, there was something going on here that they did not want the United States government to know about. Longarm was fairly sure none of them gave a shit about him in particular. It was who and what he represented that frightened them.

But how? That he couldn't figure out.

Bennett and Walker both would understand the limitations of jurisdiction, and they sure as hell knew that murder was not a federal crime.

Longarm and Will Hancock could bluster and pretend all

they pleased. The truth—and they knew it—was that those murders had occurred on lands subject to the territorial government of Wyoming and *not* on tribal ground. Longarm could investigate on the basis of their pretext, but anything he turned up would ultimately have to be prosecuted in the local court or, since that seemed unlikely as long as George Walker was the county judge, down in Cheyenne at the territorial court.

But . . . what crime? If it wasn't murder, and Longarm did not see how that could fit into Walker's worries given the facts of the legal system, just what was going on around here that Walker and Company wanted silenced so bad they would be willing to pay him three thousand dollars on the promise he would ignore it.

It didn't make sense. Yet.

It did, however, worry him to the point that he about half expected to be the target of a bullet coming out of the night as he rode from the WWW back to McCollum.

After all, if a three-thousand-dollar bribe wouldn't work, how easy would it be to lay out a lot less than that and buy an assassination.

He rode loose in the stirrups all the way back to town, ready to drop like a rock and play possum at the first glimmer of a muzzle flash, but the only excitement the whole way back was when his horse spooked a jackrabbit, which in turn scared hell out of the horse, which damn near dumped Longarm, who was riding loose in the saddle and ready to jump.

By the time that little incident was done with, Longarm wasn't sure which of them had the quickest heartbeat, him or the horse or the rabbit.

Still, no harm had been done, and he got back to town by ten-thirty or so, returned the horse to its stall in the livery stable, and hiked back to Mrs. Benson's house without anyone trying to stab, shoot, or club him.

Not that he was complaining.

And he was only about half surprised to find the old lady waiting up for him with leftovers from the supper he'd ridden off and missed. He apologized profusely, and let her fuss and fidget over him while he packed in another of her light snacks, this one not more than would've fed eight or ten hungry Indians.

Chapter 38

Longarm was groaning by the time breakfast was done the next morning. His belly actually hurt from all the food Mrs. Benson packed into it. If the old woman ever took a notion to open a boardinghouse in Denver, Longarm would be done for. He'd become fat as a hog waiting for slaughter. And the awfullest part of that would be that he would sit there and actually *help* her do it to him. The woman was such a fine cook that even when he knew better, he couldn't hardly turn down "just a dab" of this or "a little taste" of that. Lordy!

When he just couldn't take it any longer, he grabbed his hat, all three acres of it, and excused himself. "I prob'ly won't find anybody willing to talk t' me around here," he said, "but I reckon I got t' try."

"If you don't mind a word of advice from someone who doesn't know anything at all about the law, but who does know a little bit about the people who live around here, I suggest you ask your questions where there's no one else around to see or hear. The people in this county know enough to be afraid of George Walker, but that doesn't mean that everybody likes him."

Longarm surprised Mrs. Benson—and himself too, for that matter—by leaning down and planting a kiss on the old woman's cheek. "You aren't just a fine cook an' a pretty face," he said, "you're smart too. Thanks for the suggestion."

She blushed furiously, and was quite obviously pleased by the attention. That did not, however, stop her from giving him a stern warning before he could get out the front door. "Mind you're back here no later than twelve noon sharp," she said. "I already have a pot roast on the stove, and I don't want to ruin it waiting for you to get done lollygagging."

"Yes, ma'am," he responded solemnly. "I won't forget."

Damn, he thought as he headed down the street. He'd almost forgotten what it felt like to be living under his mother's iron rule. Now he remembered.

He went back to the telegraph office and got off another wire, paid for this time, telling Billy Vail where he was and requesting that more cash be sent to him. What with the deposit for the hired horse and all the things he'd had to buy since Paolo's wagon was burned up, he was about to run out of cash money again.

"I don't s'pose you've heard anything about the murders down south of here or the problems the sheepherders been having," Longarm suggested to the telegraph operator/store-keeper.

"Nope. Not a word. Would've told the sheriff if I did hear anything, though. That'd be my civic duty, right?"

"So it would."

The gent gave a grunt and a nod. "No need for you to be nosing into our business here. We take care of our own."

"Yeah, I'm sure you do at that," Longarm said. "Thanks for the help."

"You want me to come find you if your money comes through?"

"I'll drop by again this afternoon. There's no telling where I'll be until then."

The local chuckled. "Wouldn't make any difference if you know or don't. I could ask most anybody and they'd be able to tell me where you are if I need to look you up."

"Now there's a distressing thought," Longarm said.

The telegrapher shrugged. "Just the way it is in a town like this. Or you could always go home to Denver."

"I expect that I will. And soon. G'day now." Longarm touched the brim of his hat—he was getting really quite good at remembering to reach out all that distance now instead of poking the underside of the brim and knocking the silly thing askew, as he'd done more than once when he'd first started wearing it—and wandered out onto the sidewalk.

Across the street people were moving in and out of the courthouse. One of them coming out, Longarm saw, was Deputy Tim Burch. Something tugged lightly at Longarm's memory. Damn if Burch didn't look familiar to him. Sort of. Longarm was positive they'd never met. But he kind of had the idea that he might've seen Burch before, or anyway someone who looked very much like him.

Not on a wanted poster, though. That he would have remembered for sure. No, if he'd ever encountered the man before now, it would've been a casual, passing sort of thing and not something worth worrying about.

It was too early for a drink. And he might not be able to stomach so much as looking at a free-lunch counter for two weeks after he did leave McCollum, thanks to Mrs. Benson and the way she liked to feed a man. But where there was beer there were men to drink it, and tongues that might begin to wag with a little liquid encouragement. Longarm turned toward the nearest saloon with the idea in mind that he might spend a little of Billy Vail's money buying drinks for a local or two. He figured he could afford to go light in the pocket now that he knew there was more expense money on the way.

He was about halfway there when he saw that Burch had walked ahead a ways, passed over to this side of the street, and now was coming back in the direction of the telegraph office.

Longarm was not particularly anxious for a run-in with any of Mikey Bennett's people. But he was damned if he was going to step aside for any of them either.

Longarm was fully prepared to get his back up if that was what was wanted here. Instead, to his amazement, Burch dropped his chin as he came close, and as he passed Longarm uttered in a low, slightly hoarse voice, "Meet me behind the livery barn. Ten minutes."

Then Burch was gone. He hadn't once looked directly at Longarm, and anyone observing them from a distance would have had no idea that the exchange ever took place.

Hell, Longarm wasn't sure he'd heard it right, and he was the only human close enough that might have.

He walked swiftly on, careful not to turn his head or alter his gait in any way. He acted as if none of it had occurred.

When he got to the saloon that had been his original destination, he kept on walking.

Ten minutes, Burch had said. Longarm didn't have his watch with him, but he figured ten minutes would be about right for a stroll to the far end of McCollum and back again to the livery stable.

Besides, that would help walk off some of the fullness in his belly.

And give him a chance to observe whether anybody was following him or seeming to pay undue attention to his movements.

He wondered . . . then put the questions aside. Ten minutes. He'd find out then.

Chapter 39

It was not beyond the realm of possibility that this invite could be a setup. Longarm knew that. After all, last night he'd refused Judge Walker's bold-as-brass attempt to bribe a federal peace officer, and had felt at the time that he'd needed to watch his backside on his return in the dark. Longarm saw no reason to drop that vigilance now.

He walked a slow circle around the livery barn before he approached it, just to make sure there was no one waiting in ambush close by. If anyone was, they were so damn good at it that they would get away with it.

And Longarm didn't believe that any son of a bitch was that good.

Once he was satisfied that no one had been put into place with a rifle ahead of time, Longarm entered the barn. Carefully.

No one lay in wait inside either. Tim Burch was standing at the far end of the aisle that ran between the two rows of stalls inside the barn. He saw Longarm enter, and nodded, but waited patiently while Longarm checked around to make sure they were alone.

There was no sign of the livery operator. The tack room that doubled as the man's office was empty, as were the stalls. Longarm looked into each and every one of them, then climbed the ladder into the loft, and even went so far as to poke through the hay that was stacked there. The only living things he saw in the loft were a pair of small birds perched on one of the rafters and a lean and ugly yellow cat that was busy chewing on what looked like a fresh rat's tail. Working livestock, Longarm thought. He went back down the ladder, lifted the lid on the zinc-lined and supposedly rat-proof grain bin to make sure there wasn't anyone eavesdropping from in there either, then finally consented to go down the aisle and greet Burch.

"All right. What is it?"

Burch looked more than a little nervous. He kept paying more attention to the open front doors than to Longarm.

"Go in that stall there," Longarm said. "Anybody looking in from the street won't see you if that's what you're worried about."

Burch licked dry lips, looked out toward the street again, and said, "What about you?"

"Get in the stall. Nobody will pay me any mind."

Burch slipped inside a stall that contained a chestnut mare, her belly bulging with a foal that surely would be born soon. The mare seemed content to share her space with a human.

"I can see your head over the top of the rails. Sit on the feed bunk or something. And wait there. I'll be right back."

"You aren't gonna—"

"Just wait there a minute, will you?" Longarm snapped.

He left Burch hiding—seemed silly for a grown man, but what the hell did Longarm know about the way things were here—while he fetched his rented horse out of its stall further up the aisle.

He slipped a rope halter onto the animal and found some leads hanging beside the tack-room door, then used those to cross-tie the horse in the aisle, choosing a spot that amazingly enough put him right beside the spot where Deputy Burch was hiding.

Longarm found a brush, hoof pick, and curry comb inside the tack room, and took them back to where the horse was tied. A man could spend as much time as he cared to with grooming a horse, and any passersby would find nothing at all unusual in the sight of someone working on the coat and feet of a riding mount.

"Oh, yeah. Good idea," Burch said as he peeked out between the stall rails and saw what Longarm was about. "I should have thought of that."

"Doesn't matter, just so one of us did," Longarm said. "Now tell me. What is it that you're wantin' to say t' me that you'd have to hide from all your friends while you say it?"

Chapter 40

"Look, I could get fired just for talking to you. You know? But I . . . I don't want there to be no misunderstandings. That's the thing. The sheriff, he doesn't know about you. Judge Walker doesn't neither."

"And you do?" Longarm asked.

"Yeah, as a matter of fact I do," Burch said. "I grew up out east of Castle Rock."

"I know that country."

"Exactly. I know you do. Well, my folks have a little place there. Not a ranch. It's a farm. God, don't tell nobody that, will you? I'd get laughed outa the county if you told that to anybody up here. I sure never have. I'm not ashamed of it, mind. It's just, well . . ."

"I won't say anything," Longarm assured him.

"Yeah. Thanks. Anyway, I always hated farming. Staring at a mule's ass all day. You probably don't know how that is, but I sure do."

Longarm did too. And he'd hated it himself. But he said nothing to Burch about that. It was none of this young deputy's business what Custis Long's boyhood was like.

"When I was old enough to take work on my own, I went up to Denver. I used to do some odd jobs around the stockyards and out at the Diamond D. You and me know some of the same people there."

"You know Johnny Birdwell?" Longarm asked.

"I've met him. Worked some for his son Tom."

Longarm nodded, picked up the near-side forefoot of the horse, and set in to cleaning it with the steel hook of the hoof pick. "Go on."

"Anyhow, like I was trying to say, I know something about you. I mean, you're practically a legend around that part of the country."

Longarm said nothing. He didn't feel like allowing himself to be suckered in with a mite of unearned praise.

"They say you're good, Marshal. Real good. But they say you're fair too. They say you won't pick up a man for vagrancy and beat on him for sport the way the railroad police will or some of the Denver city blues. They say you'd rather give a man a dollar than put him behind bars for the night.

"And they say you aren't petty. If a guy isn't hurting anybody or if there's any way to give a man a break, they say you'll do that too.

"I know what we done to you down at the sheep wagon that time, that was petty. I know that. Roger does too. But Roger, he's petty. He flies off the handle, and he likes to show off that he's tough and he can put anybody in jail.

"I think he really did believe you were a deputy—even right then at the time, I think he believed you were who you said you were. I think he just wanted to haul you in like that to show that he could. Not so much to show you, I don't think, but to show Henry and Barry and me. Most especially, I think he wanted to do it to show off to the sheriff that he could. Roger would like to be sheriff himself someday, and the truth is he's a lot smarter than Mike Bennett is."

"And anyway," Longarm injected, "there's going to be a vacancy in the office when Walker allows Bennett to move up and become county judge."

Burch sounded startled. "How'd you know a thing like that when you practically just got here? That's supposed to be secret."

Longarm didn't answer. He figured Tim Burch could likely imagine something much more interesting than the truth, which had to do with a garrulous old woman's love of gossip and of having someone who would listen to her nattering.

"Shit, I knew you were good, Marshal Long, but—"

"Get back to what you were saying," Longarm told him.

"Right, sure. Anyway, like I was telling you, things got off on a sour note here, and nobody around this county seems to realize that instead of trying to keep you out of things, the best thing for everybody to do would be to be straight with you. They started out thinking they could bully you. Hell, I know better than that, and I'm no judge or sheriff or chief deputy even. But I know you can't bully a federal officer out of anything. Especially not somebody with a reputation like yours.

"Then they thought maybe they could buy you off. I tried to tell them different, but they don't listen to the likes of me. I'm at the bottom of the heap around here. Truth is, I been thinking about moving on. I think I've about used up my time in Warren County, and I'd leave right now except there's a girl I been sparking and I'd like to spend some more time with her. Maybe even get serious about taking her back down to Colorado and . . . I dunno . . . settling down to something decent and honest."

"Not like law enforcement," Longarm said dryly.

"Exactly," Burch responded just as serious as serious could be. But then for *him*, Longarm thought, maybe the practice of enforcing laws and protecting folks had nothing decent or honest in it.

"Go on."

"Right. I tried to tell them to just be honest with you and you'd back off. I mean, the stuff that's going on up here . . . and I don't know all of it myself or I'd tell you all . . . it's stuff that as a federal officer you wouldn't care about anyhow. I know you wouldn't mess in where you don't have jurisdiction. I've tried to explain that to them, but they don't listen. And I'm scared somebody might take this thing too far and get me crossways with you. I don't want to do that, Marshal. I'm no match for you and don't pretend to be."

"What *is* going on up here?" Longarm asked.

"Like I told you, I don't really know much about that. I mean, I know that Judge Walker has big plans for the future. Political stuff. His brother is already down in Cheyenne. He's involved in the territorial government. Pulling strings from behind the scenes. While he's doing that, the judge is running Warren County. And I mean he runs all of it. I think he's scared somebody like you will come in and shake him out of the top of the tree. Something like that. I've tried to tell them that you wouldn't give a fat crap what happens in Warren County so long as it isn't anything against federal law, but they won't listen. They just won't listen."

"Murder isn't a federal law, but don't you ever think I'd forget about that," Longarm said.

"You mean those sheepherders?"

"That's exactly who I mean, Burch, and you know it."

"You don't have to sound so mad, do you?" Burch whined.

"Rape and murder piss me off. They make me real mad."

"Rape? Marshal Long, I don't know *any*thing about anybody being raped nor who did those murders either. Believe me, I'd tell you in a heartbeat if I knew anything worth telling."

"Then tell me what you do know."

"Yeah, well, the truth is that me and Henry went down there with Roger to put the roust on those sheepherders. I mean . . . we been told to do that sort of thing. You know?"

"I know," Longarm growled.

"Look, maybe you don't see it like that, but folks up here are cow people. They hate sheep. Judge Walker most of all. He can't abide the thought of a damn sheep. So the standing rule is, if you see a sheepherder, give him some grief. And even . . . look, I'm being honest with you about this, okay? I want you to keep that in mind, Marshal."

"I'm listening," Longarm said.

"Our rule is we can shoot up the sheep and the dogs and we can beat on the herders if we like."

"If you like?"

"Okay, we're supposed to. That's the order. If we see a sheepman, we're to beat the shit out of him. Make him want to walk a hundred miles out of his way next time if he has to, but we don't want their kind . . . I mean *they,* the judge and them . . . don't want that kind in Warren County."

"What happened down south went way the hell past a beating," Longarm said.

"I know that. But the thing is, we didn't do that. We saw the wagon and the sheep and we went over there to have a little fun. I mean, we would have shot some sheep and beat the old man and everything. We was supposed to do that. Then you got into the scrape with Roger, and we brought you back to town here to put you in jail. But you saw that we didn't hurt the old man or that girl. We didn't."

"And over the next couple days?" Longarm asked. "Where'd you go while I was in that jail cell?"

"We had some warrants to serve over around Howards. It took us most of the time to do that. Then on the way back, we thought we'd swing down and take up where we'd left off with those sheepherders. But we never . . . we never killed anybody there, Marshal. And we damn sure never raped that girl. If we'd caught her we might've stripped and whipped her. I'll be honest with you about that. Roger was talking about putting some stripes on her back. But . . . when we found the wagon it was already burning and the old man was dead. So were those dogs and a bunch of the sheep."

"And the girl?"

"There wasn't any sign of her. She was gone. So was whoever killed the man. We never saw who that was."

"But you didn't do anything about it?" Longarm said, his voice harsh now and his expression cold.

"We . . . dammit, Marshal, Roger said they was only sheepherders, after all. The man was dead. Wasn't anything we could do about it then. And Roger . . . for that matter the judge and the sheriff too . . . wouldn't want to cause trouble for a cattleman just because he had sense enough to hate sheep. And mind, we didn't know about the girl then. We didn't see anything of her.''

"You didn't think about what might've happened to her?" Longarm demanded.

"Well, sure. But we didn't think . . . didn't think anybody would rape and kill her. That isn't civilized.''

"No, I'd have to agree that it ain't,'' Longarm said.

"What we did think about and talk about at the time was that you were up here in the jail and would likely want to take a hand in this. And I told the other boys how good you are. Roger, I think he's about half scared of you. Which I guess he ought to be. He made his brag and he took it all too far, and now here we were sitting there looking at a murdered man, and Roger got to worrying that you'd try to pin the killing on him. On us, that is. And Roger said we were to ride back here to McCollum and not say a word to anybody. We weren't to report the killing, not even to Mike or the judge, and we were to keep our mouths shut and make like we didn't know a thing about any of it, or else you would be making trouble and maybe get the three of us fired or charged with murder even. Roger told us not to tell anybody. And I haven't. Not until this minute.

"But dammit, Marshal, they just won't listen to me. You aren't the sort to charge a man just because you want to get back at him about something else. That's what Roger is afraid of. He thinks you're gonna have it in for him and go after him regardless. Me, I know better. And that's why I wanted you to know the truth about this. That's why I wanted to talk to you today. All right?''

"All right,'' Longarm said. "We've talked.''

"And you'll leave us be? Please?''

"We've talked. I thank you for the information. Whatever comes from here on, Burch, I'll remember what you've told me.''

"I've been honest as I know how, Marshal. I haven't held nothing back. We were there, it's true. We saw what happened to that sheepherder and we didn't report it or try and find out who did do it. But we never killed anybody and we damn sure never raped that girl. I want you to know that, Marshal. There's things I'll do for my pay, but there's limits. Straight-out murder is more than I want to get involved in. Raping a virgin girl, that's way the hell past my limit. I wouldn't do that for all the judge's money. I want you to know that, Marshal, and I want you to keep in mind that I've been straight with you here today. Just if . . . you know. Just in case."

"I won't forget a word you've said, Burch," Longarm promised.

Longarm concentrated on grooming the horse, his back to the stall where Tim Burch was hiding. After a moment he heard the stall gate creak on its hinges and the sound of the latch. The next time Longarm turned around, the stall was empty save for the pregnant mare, and Burch was gone, slipped out the back of the barn and away, presumably without anyone seeing him.

Longarm finished with the horse's feet and began giving it a final going-over with the soft dandybrush.

Chapter 41

"Now you just pick that napkin up, young man, and put it back on your lap where it belongs."

"I couldn't hold another bite. Honestly."

"Of course you can. Didn't I tell you the blackberry cobbler would be out of the oven soon? You aren't going anywhere until you've had a taste of my special cobbler."

"Mrs. Benson, I couldn't—"

"Of course you can. Now do as I say."

Longarm stood, folded his napkin, and laid it carefully beside his plate. He bent and gave the woman a light peck on the cheek. She smelled of scented talcum. "It will taste better when it's had a little while to breathe," he said. "I'll stop back in for a snack this afternoon." He thought, but did not add, if I can still walk after this lunch.

"You promise?"

"Promise."

"All right then. But I will expect you at three. We will have the cobbler then. And some tea. I think tea would be just right with it, don't you?"

"Just right," he agreed, reaching for his hat.

It would be wasteful to discard a perfectly good hat like this and squander government expense money on yet another

153

one. Sure was tempting, though. Perhaps at the Main Street Mercantile?

"Sorry, mister. Your money hasn't shown up yet. Won't until they find whatever is wrong with the wire and get it fixed. But don't worry. By now they're sure to know the line is down. Somebody is sure to already be out looking to take care of the problem."

"Again?" Longarm complained. "Damn, but you seem to be down most of the time here."

The telegraph operator gave him a quizzical look. "Mister, we don't hardly ever go down anymore. Used to real often, of course, before they cleaned the buffalo out of this part of the country. Damn buffalo would use the telegraph poles to rub against. You get six or seven thousand buffalo pushing and rubbing and butting at things, and they could knock down miles of wire at a time. But we're hardly ever silent nowadays."

It was Longarm's turn to look puzzled. "You were down just a couple days ago, weren't you?"

"Days? You must be thinking of some other place. My key hasn't been closed since . . . let me think . . . last April, I think it was. Had a late storm come through with real wet snow that hung on the wire and turned to ice. We were down more than a week that time. But service between here and Cheyenne hasn't been interrupted since that April blizzard."

"You're sure about that?"

"Of course I'm sure. I'm the only operator in McCollum. Damn right I'd know if I can transmit or not."

"Now mister, that is just about as interesting as it can be," Longarm said.

The telegraph operator shrugged and said, "Anything else I can do for you?"

"No, you've already been a big help, thanks."

"Check back with me tomorrow morning. I might have something for you then. Your message did get out all right, though. The Cheyenne operator receipted for it, so your answer should be back soon as they get the wire fixed.''

"Thanks. Thanks a *lot*."

Longarm spun around and stalked away from the mercantile.

Interesting, by God. Damn well interesting and getting the more so all the time.

Chapter 42

Longarm entered the courthouse and climbed to the second floor, to Sheriff Michael Bennett's office and the adjoining jail. It did not feel like a homecoming.

"Something I can help you with?" the flatulent jailer said.

"You have a deputy working here named Barry, I believe."

"That's right. Barry Daniels."

"I'd like to talk t' him. Any idea where I might find him?"

"Him and the other deputies went over to the Fox Den, I think."

Longarm raised an eyebrow.

"It's a saloon. They serve pretty good meals there too. Chops, stews, like that. Block and a half east from here."

"All right, thanks." Longarm considered giving the old fart a present. A hat. Might've done it, except that would mean he'd have to buy a new one, and he couldn't afford that until the problem with the telegraph wire was fixed. He went back downstairs and turned east. The Fox Den was indistinguishable from any other hole-in-the-wall saloon except for a sign hung out front depicting a large black blob—presumably the hole leading into an underground den—and a very badly drawn fox done in red barn paint. McCollum, he reflected, would tear the heart out of anyone with an artistic bent.

Among the customers gathered inside the Fox Den for an early, and wet, lunch were Warren County deputies Roger Donnington, Henry Adair, and Barry Daniels. Tim Burch was not with them. The three were crouched around a small table with their faces practically touching the greasy-looking but actually rather good-smelling bowls of what looked to be green chili.

Chili verde properly done was most likely the dish the ancient Greeks had in mind when they talked about "nectar of the gods," or so Longarm figured. There was a restaurant in Denver that . . . he quit thinking about how good the chili smelled. He'd promised Mrs. Benson to be back at the boardinghouse in time for the cobbler and tea, and would hurt her feelings bad if he didn't show up.

Speaking of which . . . "Got the time, mister?" Longarm asked the Fox Den's bartender.

The man pointed to a large Regulator clock hanging on a side wall. Twenty till two. Longarm had plenty of time to get back to the house before the old landlady's deadline of straight-up three.

"Thanks."

Across the room the three local deputies were pointedly *not* staring at Longarm. They were being so obvious about pretending that they didn't know he was there that it was kinda funny. Or would have been if this whole shitty situation wasn't so serious.

Longarm wandered over their way, and when they were pretty well forced to admit that he was standing there, he nodded to them.

"Something you want, Long?" Donnington demanded.

Longarm didn't answer immediately. He pulled out the vacant fourth chair at the table and helped himself to a seat. "Smells good," he said.

"It is good. Is that what you came here for? A recommendation about what to have for lunch?"

"Nope. But when I saw you boys I noticed Deputy Daniels' boots. Mighty nice. Fancy."

Daniels actually grinned and bobbed his head and seemed quite pleased with what he took to be a compliment. "They are, aren't they? I had them made up special by mail order. Gent down in San Angelo, Texas, made them for me. What you do is you stand on a piece of paper, see, and have some-one take a pencil or charcoal and draw the shape of your foot. Then this bootmaker—he's awful good—he'll make up boots that fit you perfect. Make any style you want."

The deputy turned slightly and stuck a foot out so Longarm could better see the fancy stitching and excellent workman-ship. "The foot part is made of regular leather, but the upper parts there are snakeskin. Handsome, ain't it?"

"Sure is," Longarm agreed. "Isn't that pointy toe uncom-fortable, though?"

"Not at all. It looks sharp"—he laughed at his own sort-of joke—"but it feels the same as any boot. Didn't he do a good job for me?"

"Sure did."

"I can find his address for you if you want."

"Thanks, but I expect I'll stick with my old boots. I like a heel built for walking, not one of those undershot deals."

Daniels said, "He'll make them up with any kind of heel you want. Any toe style. All sorts of materials and decorative stitching. I got a catalog from him if you want to see it."

"Thanks. I'll let you know."

"Is that all you're bothering us about, Long?" Donnington asked.

Longarm smiled at him. "This may amaze you, Roger, but in fact that *is* the only thing I wanted." He stood, waving away the waiter who'd headed in his direction. "Enjoy your lunch, boys. I expect I'll be seeing all of you again real soon."

He turned and strode quickly outside.

Chapter 43

"Marshal Long! Over here. Can I speak with you for a moment, please."

It took Longarm a second to see who was speaking to him and where she was sitting. The woman's voice came from inside a carriage that was parked inside an alley in the next block toward town from Mrs. Benson's boardinghouse. A man—more kid than man really—was sitting on the driver's bench.

Longarm hadn't seen the lady at first because the side curtains, heavy black curtains designed more for privacy than protection from rain or snow, had been set in place on the door, and roller shades had been drawn over the glass windows in the handsome rig.

The team standing quiet in harness to pull the carriage was an exceptionally fine pair of blood bays, as perfectly matched as any twins could be, and with the broad chests and classic head shapes that spoke of quality bloodlines running back for generations.

"Come inside with me, please." The carriage door swung open, and Longarm could see the voice belonged to the girl he'd last seen in George Walker's study out at the WWW.

She motioned for Longarm to climb into the carriage, then poked her head out and said to the driver, "Go across the street, Leonard, and wait over there. Come back when you see the gentleman leave.''

''Yes, ma'am.'' The boy's answer was so pathetically eager to please that Longarm had to figure he was smitten with the girl. Well, there wasn't anything odd about that. She was one damn-all fine-looking filly. And likely no older than her driver. Just a hell of a lot better off due to her position as Walker's . . . as whatever she was to George Walker.

Longarm didn't have any part of that straight. Daughter, protégé, wife, mistress. She could've been any of those. Or for that matter, a combination among them. For sure now, she was living with style and power.

The driver jumped down, nodded briefly to Longarm, and trotted obediently out of range so he couldn't overhear anything that might be said inside that carriage.

''Are you coming?'' she prompted.

There were a couple of responses he could have made to a question that broadly open to interpretation. All he did, though, was remove his hat—not only was that the polite thing to do, he wasn't sure it would fit through the door width if he tried to keep it on—and climb inside. The girl pulled the door closed behind him, and fussily made sure the latch was set so the carriage door could not swing open again by accident.

After the full glare of midday sunlight, the inside of the coach was dark and airless. Longarm was acutely conscious of the scent of the girl's perfume.

Couldn't help but be conscious of other things about her either. Like the fact that she was so almighty nice to look at.

As she had the first time he'd seen her on the street beside the courthouse, she wore her long black hair loose and brushed to a gloss. Unlike that first time, he saw that she was smiling at him.

''What brings you here?'' he asked.

''You do,'' she told him boldly.

''How's that again?''

''I was waiting here for you. Someone mentioned you were staying with Mrs. Benson. Isn't she a dear?''

160

"Yeah, a dear. That's exactly how I'd've put it too."

"Don't make fun of me. I mean it. I like Mrs. Benson. And I like you too."

"Really? I hadn't noticed that before. Not that there's been all that much opportunity t' think about it."

"I've been thinking about you, though. Ever since I saw you on the street that day." She laughed. "With your face pressed up against the backside of that horse and your wrists in irons."

"It was one o' my better moments, it's true. Thanks for reminding me."

"Oh, I'm only teasing. A little." She leaned forward and very lightly touched the shelf of his jaw, then ran a fingertip up the side of his face, across his forehead, and down to the other side of his jaw. That faint touch of hers felt as if it was charged with static electricity. "You're handsome," she said.

"You're pretty."

"I told you, I've been thinking about you."

"Yes?"

"I want you."

"Just like that?"

"Yes. Just like that."

"And in just what way d'you find yourself wanting me?"

She laughed again. Threw her head back and then gave him a coquettish smile. Her only answer was not in words. She slid forward to the very edge of the carriage seat to give herself more room to move her limbs, then swiftly undid the buttons that held her bodice together.

She was not wearing anything beneath her shirtwaist. Her upper body was perfect, her skin like velvet, and her breasts with that firm, taut structure that comes only with youth. She had nipples that were pale and exceptionally small set daintily atop breasts that were just right for a handful.

She did something with the buttons and buckles at her waist, and her skirt opened on one side and was allowed to fall away. She wore nothing under that either. She shrugged out of the

161

blouse and sat there in the carriage, naked save for the smile that she showed him.

"Does that explain it?" she asked.

"Ayuh. I think so."

She leaned forward and unfastened his trousers, helped him shove them down, and without even giving Longarm time to kick his boots off or step out of the britches that were bunched around his ankles, pulled him on top of her there inside the close and stuffy confinement of George Walker's carriage.

The girl was young, but there wasn't anything about her that was inexperienced. She was wet, receptive, and as hot as a firecracker on Chinese New Year.

She clamped her legs around his waist, her arms around his chest, and her teeth on his ear, and clung to him as tight as a cowboy riding out a bad horse on a frosty morning.

Longarm was half tempted to holler yahoo and dig his spurs in. And if he'd done it, he doubted that the damn girl would've minded. She was quivering and churning, grinding her hips and slapping his hard, hairy belly with her pale soft one.

It was hot inside the carriage, and soon the sounds of skin slapping against skin turned wet.

Longarm didn't mind.

He hadn't thought he was all that horny. But then he'd been spending time mostly with Mrs. Benson the past few days.

Now that he found himself hip-deep inside this pretty girl's body, he expected he could work up a dab of interest in the subject.

He could feel the sap rising deep in his balls and the wild, wonderful feeling every time he plunged himself into and onto her.

The feelings gathered until they couldn't be held back any longer, and his whole body stiffened and went rigid as he threw himself into her with one final, convulsive thrust.

The girl cried out in response, and clutched at him with a fierce and sudden strength as she bit the pad of muscle on his shoulder and, gasping, fell back away from him onto the now-sweat-slick upholstery of the carriage seat.

162

"Damn," he said in a voice that came out almost in a croak. "You surely do know how t' tell a fella you'd like to get t' know him better."

She laughed, then leaned forward again. She took his wet cock in her hand and played with it for a moment, wiping the juices that remained there onto her palm and fingers. And then, her eyes locked on his, she slowly and deliberately raised that hand to her mouth and licked the spent cum from it.

"Tonight," she said.

"What about tonight?"

"I want to do this again. Tonight. You know where I live."

"Yes, but d'you think our friend George would mind me droppin' by to rip a piece off your pretty ass."

"Don't be crude, please."

"Sorry," he said, not particularly meaning it.

"Tonight I want you to meet me. There is an old shack on the ranch about a mile and a half west of the house. They tell me it used to be a line shack, whatever that is. It's empty now, but there is still a bed in it. I happen to know the bed has a clean mattress and fresh hay filling it."

"You just happen t' know that, do you?"

"I told you, don't be crude. I have . . . large appetites. The judge cannot satisfy all of them. And I do not tell him quite everything that I do."

"I see."

"Meet me at the shack tonight. After dark. Say . . . eleven o'clock?"

"I've always been particularly fond o' that time."

She smiled and inserted one lovely finger into her mouth, sucking on it prettily and smiling all the while. "So have I, dear. So have I." Once she was done being seductive, her expression changed with the suddenness of a lamp being blown out. She sorted out her clothes, pulling them on and buttoning and buckling everything with the swiftness of much practice. "Eleven o'clock then?"

"Sure," Longarm said as he finished the necessary buttoning and buckling of his own clothes.

"Please tell Leonard he can come back now and drive me home."

"Be glad to," Longarm said. He climbed back out of the wagon and motioned the boy forward from his post across the street. "The lady would like to drive back t' the ranch now."

Leonard gave Longarm a look so hard, Longarm thought maybe he oughta duck out of the way. Jealous. Not that Longarm could blame him. The boy was deep in the throes of what he more than likely mistook as love for this good-looking, loose-moraled girl, but had had to stand by while another man fucked her. That'd be a hard thing to put up with, as Longarm understood full well. Hell, he'd been young once himself. Never quite that innocent maybe, but young. Poor damn kid.

Leonard drove the girl away with a snap of his whip and a shout. Longarm hoped the boy didn't take his frustration out on the team. They hadn't done anything to deserve it. The one who needed the whipping was the girl, not the horses.

And Walker, of course.

Just how fucking stupid did these people seem to think he was anyway?

Surely they didn't think he would fall for this. Shit, he wasn't entirely unpopular with the ladies, that was true. But lust at first sight? Or second or whenever? Damn girl had thought he was scum that first time she saw him. Was he supposed to have forgotten that?

And he was supposed to think she could have an assignation right there inside the judge's carriage, in broad daylight in the middle of the day, right there in town, with Leonard watching and anyone else who happened by to see the damn coach rocking and bouncing on its springs . . . all that and Longarm was supposed to believe it would be kept a deep dark secret from George Walker?

Lordy, he hoped he wasn't as dumb as this crowd seemed to insist that he was.

But tonight, he thought, ought to be mighty interesting indeed.

A sudden thought struck him, and a pang of remorse shot through him.

He began to extend his stride as he hurried on.

It'd been almost two when he'd left the damn saloon. No telling how far past Mrs. Benson's appointed time for cobbler and tea he'd strayed now. Damned if he wasn't going to be in for it when he got back.

Chapter 44

It took him most of the rest of the afternoon to find the just-right spot for what he wanted. The whole thing would have been easier if he'd taken the horse out, but that would have tipped the deal. Besides, a horse is so awfully damned difficult to hide.

So he walked. And walked. And then walked some more.

What he wanted was a place where he could make himself comfortable and stay out of sight. A place where he could be reasonably certain no one was trying to creep up behind him. And most importantly, a place along a string-straight line between the old line camp and George Walker's WWW headquarters.

The easy thing to do, of course, would be to arrive early and lay up inside the shack.

But then he figured any sensible soul would have that possibility figured out and guard against it.

And Longarm gave Walker credit for being at least fairly sensible. A son of a bitch, sure, but not an entirely stupid one . . . which Walker and his people seemed to insist that Longarm was.

That bullshit earlier in the day with . . . what the hell was the girl's name anyway? He couldn't recall ever hearing it.

Had he? He shook his head. If he had, it didn't stick in mind now.

Anyway, that was pure crap about her being so passionate that she couldn't hold herself back, she just had to have his dick inside her.

Sure. That sort of thing happens just all the time to practically everybody. Right!

Longarm believed that just as quick as he believed every claim made by a traveling snake-oil salesman: not damn likely.

The girl was there on the instruction of George Walker, no doubt about it, and the intent of both was to set Longarm's ass up for mayhem of one sort or another.

They were afraid of him. They were afraid of federal controls. And they wanted him to either back away on his own or be taken out the hard way.

When bribery failed, he guessed they'd decided that hard was the only way there was left to go.

Soften him up with Tim Burch's phony-as-hell "confession" this morning.

Confession, hell. Oh, Burch had been pretty good at it really. He might've been convincing except for a couple things, the most glaring of them being his comment about the killers raping a virgin Paula.

Paula'd been a tough little gal, tough talking and tough acting and more than a little provocative in the way she dressed and flashed her charms for men to almost but not quite see.

Longarm himself wouldn't have believed Paula Laxha was a virgin. Not until her last dying words to him, he hadn't. But she had been. And Tim Burch knew it.

Longarm would've bet his last nickel, though, that Burch wasn't the one who'd got to take Paula's cherry out there on the grass. Longarm would've laid his money on that honor falling to Roger Donnington. Donnington was the leader of Mikey Bennett's tame deputies, and had ambitions of leadership himself. No, Longarm was sure it would have been Donnington who'd claimed for himself the privilege of being the first man inside poor Paula.

Burch would've gone no better than second. Him and the third man, Barry Daniels.

And Longarm remembered now seeing Henry Adair in the office during the period when Longarm was in jail and the deputies were free to go about their marauding and raping.

Adair had been part of the group that went looking for sheep and found Custis Long along for the walk, but Adair hadn't gone back south with them after they'd brought Longarm to the jail in town.

Longarm wondered about that. Whether Adair had balked at the idea of murder and rape, or whether it was just Daniels's turn to participate in the fun they'd planned as soon as Longarm was out of the way and they were safe to return to Paolo's sheep camp.

Longarm had to figure that some parts of Tim Burch's story were taken from the truth. Certainly he knew about Longarm from a genuine Denver connection. The man's knowing Johnny and Tom pointed to that clearly enough. What Longarm now suspected was that Burch not only knew of him, but had seen him before. Likely had recognized Longarm at the sheep camp that day down south and had warned the others against starting something in which a federal officer would either have to be killed too or left alive to give testimony against them. And probably none of them would've wanted to take on that kind of responsibility without checking with the sheriff and Judge Walker beforehand.

That would be why Donnington had deliberately provoked a fight and used that as an excuse to place Longarm under arrest, knowing full well who and what he was.

Everything else after that point had just grown out of those first decisions.

And out of the mean and ugly viciousness of killing Paolo Laxha and his daughter.

By now, Longarm figured, they believed they had only one way to keep him from digging out the truth and, worse, doing something about it.

By now he believed they had determined to kill him too.

Likely they would plan to ambush him at one of two spots tonight. Either at the livery stable when he went to collect his horse so he could make the eleven o'clock rendezvous with the girl, or at the old line shack where he was supposed to think she would be waiting for him.

Like hell she'd be waiting there.

Longarm figured about the only thing he could look forward to being offered tonight would be the front end of a shotgun or something else equally lethal.

Well, surprise, surprise, boys, he silently told them.

He enjoyed the scent of wet pussy at least as well as the next man, and his pecker thumped with joy every time he caught that odor the same as anyone else's.

But he damn sure didn't think with his prick, and he wasn't going to let a little stray horniness override common sense and plain precaution.

No, sir.

By the middle of a very hot afternoon, U.S. Deputy Marshal Custis Long had himself a cozy little hidey-hole picked out, and was waiting there like a big-ass spider to see who came along and dropped into his web.

Chapter 45

Either they were laying all their wager on the line shack, or they had Bennett and maybe Adair covering the livery, because all three of the killers were there to make up for their initial error in leaving Longarm alive.

They came along shortly before sundown, probably believing that even if Longarm wanted to set up his own ambush at the line shack, he would wait until after dark to do so to avoid being seen on his way in.

Donnington, Burch, and Daniels obviously intended to be there before him no matter how early he chose to arrive.

And as an added precaution, they didn't ride out on horseback, but used the same carriage the girl had been in earlier.

No sign of poor Leonard this time, though. Daniels, pointy-toed boots and all, was on the driver's bench, while Donnington and Burch rode in back. The side curtains had been removed to allow some air to flow through, and Longarm could see the two passengers as they rolled past, raising a swirl of pale dust in the slanting late-afternoon light.

Longarm let them go by unmolested, and waited until he was sure they had time enough to take up their chosen posts before he moved silent as winter mist to join them.

Will Hancock's tribal policeman Crooked Foot was better than Longarm when it came to a quiet sneak. That did not mean that Longarm was no good at it, just that Crooked Foot was a mite better.

It was dark by the time Longarm reached the shack, and the moon would not clear the horizon for several hours yet. There was plenty of time for what Longarm wanted to do.

He dropped to all fours—glad for the first time that he wasn't encumbered by the awkward bulk of a rifle or carbine—and moved closer.

The carriage was parked bold as brass in front of the shack, which was half dugout and the other half rotting, weathermelted sod house. The carriage was to assure him that his lady love was present, he supposed.

They wouldn't all be inside. He could be sure about that. He guessed one indoors and the other two posted somewhere out front where they would be able to see him approach the doorway, which was the only way in or out. There were no windows or other doors, only the one way in.

And since they hadn't had time to prepare any holes to hide in, they would have to be using what was already there in order to gain cover.

That narrowed the choices considerably. Longarm had looked the place over early in the afternoon, and had already discovered there were only three possible places for the two outside men to hide.

One of those, of course, would be inside the wagon. He doubted they would choose that because the logical thing for anyone coming in would be to first take a look inside the wagon, just to guard against the very sort of ambush that was laid here.

Which left exactly two.

Longarm felt confident that those spots would be occupied now, and that the Warren County deputies were right this moment prepared to make an "arrest."

They would wait until he got to the door of the shack so he would be in full silhouette for whoever was inside. Let the inside man be the first to open fire. Then the outside pair would let loose with their cannons, shooting him in the back while the inside man riddled his belly.

Effective. If he allowed it to happen like that.

Longarm looped around wide so as to approach the shack with the crumbled boards of the old well casing kept between himself and the wagon. It was the outside pair that he had to worry about now. The man indoors wouldn't be able to see anything or hear very much until or unless there was someone right there in the doorway.

When he got within fifty yards of the now-dry well, Longarm dropped to his belly and slithered closer and ever closer.

Chapter 46

Ah, yes. There he was, just exactly where Longarm'd figured he should be.

Daniels it was, lying snug against the base of the well casing. Longarm could see who it was quite plainly enough even in the dark. At the moment, Longarm was close enough to reach out and feel of the fancy stitching of the boots if he so took the notion.

Likely, he thought, it would be Donnington inside where he could have the pleasure of the first shot.

That would make Burch the other outdoor man. If, that is, all the supposing was accurate.

So far, it was playing by the script Longarm had worked out in his mind this afternoon, though. So far, it was rolling along just the way he'd figured.

He eased slowly as growing grass smack up alongside Barry Daniels, palmed his Colt and reversed it in his hand, then reached out and gave Daniels a whack on the back of the head hard enough to split rock.

Daniels grunted and dropped facedown in the dirt like a stunned shoat.

"You're under arrest, you sonuvabitch," Longarm whispered almost too faintly for the sound to reach his own ears.

One down, two t' go, he reminded himself as he relieved Daniels of his long gun. That proved to be a sawed-off shotgun with twin tubes. Longarm eased it open and checked to see that it was loaded—it'd be damn-all embarrassing to find that it wasn't if he happened to need the use of it directly—and eased the breach shut again with a wince at the distinctive noise.

With any sort of luck, he figured, Burch would assume Daniels was checking his own weapon, if Burch heard at all. Donnington couldn't possibly hear it from inside the shack, Longarm figured.

Longarm rolled onto his back and peered at the ceiling of light cloud that drifted overhead. There were not enough clouds to obscure the stars that were the only source of light at the moment, and there didn't look to be any more upwind that would be worth waiting for. The visibility was as short now as he could expect it to be for quite some time, and if he waited too long, the moon would come up to the horizon and brighten things a hell of a lot more than these stars were doing.

All of which boiled down to the fact that he wasn't going to gain a damn thing by lying here in the protection of the well casing. Sooner or later he was going to have to go out there onto the hard, flat ground where there was no cover at all and where Burch could see him.

The prospect of that was somewhat less than thrilling, but putting things off wasn't going to make them a lick better.

Longarm eased back away from Daniels's limp and unconscious form, and once more began to make a wide swing, this one a quarter circle that would bring him around to have the body of the carriage between himself and the shack. From that angle, he figured, the only one awake to see him come would be Burch, and Burch should—or so Longarm did most earnestly hope—be waiting for Longarm to reach the shack door before opening fire.

He gave the trip out away from the well his very best belly-crawl, but once clear of the area, he came up onto his feet and moved in at a crouch.

There was light enough that he could be seen like that, of course.

But then he was supposed to be seen. Burch would be in a good spot to watch from, and with no cover to hide behind, there was no way for Longarm to approach his position without him observing Longarm come in.

So the hell with it. Longarm set his sneaking skills to half throttle and allowed himself to be seen.

A prickle of rising hair caused an itch on the back of his neck, and he could feel icy chills roam up and down his spine when he was sure he should be in Burch's sights, but still, there was no better way to do this. Sweat, cold and greasy, formed in his armpits and trickled down across his ribs. No, sir, he didn't much like this at all.

He feigned a ham-handed and clumsy sort of caution as he came in, acutely aware that Tim Burch should have him in his gun sights by now.

He figured Donnington's script would call for him to peek inside the carriage, so that was where he headed first.

Burch, of course, would be of the mistaken belief that Daniels was watching too from twenty yards away.

Longarm stood fully upright once he was beside the carriage. He moved to it and stood on the iron step, giving his weight to the springs and rocking the carriage body as he did so, so he could look inside.

Once he was safely there, too close for a rifle or shotgun to be brought to bear, he pulled the carriage door open and stepped inside.

He used the muzzles of the shotgun to rap lightly on the treated canvas of the carriage roof.

"Psst! Tim, ol' buddy. You're under arrest," Longarm said softly.

The result was pretty much the same as taking a stick and poking it inside a hornet's nest.

Kind of a short stick at that.

Chapter 47

Tim Burch shrieked, the pent-up tension inside him released in one squeal at the feel of a gun barrel nudging his belly from below.

He was supposed to be the one in hiding here, dammit. The pigeon down below wasn't supposed to suspect any of this.

Except it didn't work like that.

Burch's howl of startled terror woke the horses, and they, tethered only by a few pounds of lead at the end of a hitch weight, bolted forward in their own terrorized response.

Inside the coach Longarm was flung off his feet, sprawling onto the backseat of the rig, while up above Tim Burch began hollering, "Help, help, he's got me, help!"

Burch had presence of mind enough to drag out a gun and commence shooting, aiming his bullets straight downward into the middle of the carriage where Longarm had been moments earlier. But now Longarm was lying half on and half off the backseat, so Burch's shots missed him. But Longarm had faith that if he gave Burch enough chances to shoot him, eventually a bullet was bound to find its mark.

That was not a prospect that Longarm favored, so he considered that he had only one good option left. He eared back the twin hammers of the shotgun and let one charge of buckshot rip through the carriage roof toward the front, then moved his aim a few feet to the rear and triggered the second barrel.

Burch screamed again, this time in pain, and Longarm saw a dark form fly off the roof and land with a thump on the ground.

By then the horses were in full flight. Longarm did not especially want to go with them in a panic-driven nighttime runaway. He flung the door of the carriage open and threw himself through it, dropping his shoulder to roll as he landed.

The momentum of the speed the horses had built up carried him through a complete roll and onto his feet again, but too fast for his legs to catch up with. He took a tumble face-forward, and ended up skidding across entirely too much gravel and entirely too damn little grass before he was able to stop and turn, coming to his knees and snatching his Colt out of the holster. He had no idea what had become of the shotgun. He'd kind of lost track of it for a moment there. Not that it mattered anyway. Damn thing was empty now, and he hadn't gone through Daniels's pockets to find more shells.

He could hear the horses thundering off into the night. God knows where they'd wind up and when, or if, they would wander home.

Between himself and the shack he could see a dark, motionless lump that would be Burch.

Live or dead, he couldn't be sure, so he approached with a considerable degree of caution, his Colt held ready to use at the slightest hint of movement.

He needed have worried. Tim Burch wasn't going to be doing any more moving. Not under his own power, he wasn't.

The shotgun blast had ripped most of his face away. His head, what was left of it, lay in a pool of blood that gleamed black in the starlight.

No, Tim Burch from Castle Rock wasn't going anywhere at all from here.

As for Roger Donnington . . . Longarm had no idea why Roger was being so quiet.

Longarm stood, his knee joints creaking, and rubbed the palms of his hands one by one on his jeans to wipe them clean of sweat and grit and the sticky blood that was oozing from some scrapes he'd picked up in his rather undignified exit from the carriage.

"It's just you and me now, Roger. You might as well come out."

He waited, but there was no response.

"Okay, I give up. You ain't in there after all. My mistake," Longarm said loudly into the night air. "Good thing the place is empty, because I'm fixing to do the same thing I'm sure you expected to do was I to hole up inside, Roger. I'm fixing to set that roof on fire. Have you got a good look at it lately? I did. This afternoon. Not much sod left. Mostly dry grass and sun-dried timbers. It'll burn hot and quick, Roger. But you do whatever you're of a mind to. And hell, if you ain't in there at all, then I guess the joke's on me, right?"

"You son of a bitch, Long."

"Care to surrender yourself, Roger? I'll take you in easy if you let me."

"No damn way, Long."

"You'd get a fair trial. I can promise you that."

"It isn't the trial that worries me. It's prison after. You got any idea what they'd do to me in there? A deputy? And after raping that girl too? I wouldn't last a week inside, and we both know it."

"Hell of a time t' be thinking about that, ain't it?" Longarm drawled.

There was another long pause. Then Donnington called, "I'm coming out, Long. Don't shoot."

"Come ahead," Longarm responded. "You got your chance." As soon as the last sound was out of his mouth, he moved quietly aside. He did not want to be standing in that same position when Donnington showed himself.

Donnington did not come out shooting, though. Longarm had to give the man credit for that small amount of courage anyway. He stepped outside into the clear night air and stood there for a moment, squared off to face Longarm, his gun in its holster and his hands held at his sides.

"You ready, Long?"

"Any time you want, or not at all if you'll drop the belt and let me put cuffs on you. Though if you don't mind, I'd have t' borrow yours. Mine are back in Denver. Part of the charade about being a camp helper, you understand."

"I can't let you take me in, Long. I couldn't stand what those bastards would do to me in there." He grinned. "Besides, who says you can take me. I figure to come out of this easy."

"You still have the choice, Roger. Drop the belt, and I'll take you in for a fair trial."

"Naw. I'm faster than you anyhow."

"You'll have to prove it."

"I guarantee it," Roger Donnington declared.

He was wrong.

Chapter 48

Longarm had no way to carry the dead. No way to carry himself, for that matter. The carriage and team of bays were long since gone and could be miles away by now, and Longarm had walked all the way out from town in the afternoon.

He dragged the bodies inside the shack, Tim Burch and Roger Donnington both, and used Barry Daniels's own handcuffs to immobilize him before searching him for weapons and his handcuff key and then waking the man.

"You're gonna have to walk back to town," Longarm said.

"You can't make me do that, damn you."

"Well, I s'pose you're right about that. Reckon I can't force you t' walk if you don't want to, and I got no horse or wagon to haul you back in. Turn around an' let me unlock those manacles, will you?"

"You're letting me go?"

"Shit, no, I won't let you go. But it wouldn't look right if you was found with your wrists in iron an' a bullet in you."

Daniels turned pale. He also walked back to McCollum.

Longarm deposited Daniels in the jail, to the great consternation of the jailer, who blustered, "I'm going to have to tell the sheriff about this."

"You go right ahead an' do that, friend. But let me mention

one thing to you. You turn your key and let this son of a bitch out on the street again, I won't only find him and put him inside, you'll already be in a cell waiting for him. You understand me? I'm taking full responsibility for what I'm doing here, but I'm taking full authority along with it. As of now an' until you hear otherwise from the territorial attorney general's office down in Cheyenne, I'm taking charge of all law enforcement in this county. Am I makin' myself clear?"

"Yes, sir. That's nice and clear."

"Good. Now tell me where the telegrapher lives."

"He doesn't work at night, Marshal, he—"

"He's gonna work this night, dammit. Now tell me where I can find him."

"Yes, sir. You go down two blocks and . . ."

Michael Bennett was more than a little bit pissed off. It took no special powers of observation to see that. He came boiling into town in the middle of the night, brought his horse to a hock-dragging stop in front of the courthouse, and came tearing up the steps to find Longarm seated in an armchair and Deputy Henry Adair behind the sheriff's own desk.

"Who the hell do you think you are?" Bennett roared.

"I'm the fella that is gonna put you behind bars down at the territorial penitentiary," Longarm told him. "I've already got wires off to my boss in Denver and to a friend o' mine in Cheyenne. Maybe you know him. Jim Doyle, assistant attorney general for the territory. I've already given them a rough idea o' what we got here.

"Been having a nice chat with Henry here too. You should've listened to him when he told you to lay off. The only thing that I question is whether Judge Walker really didn't know that Donnington and your other deputies intended to rape and murder that girl. Henry says Walker's plan was to kill sheep, not people, so he could make a name for himself in the Cattleman's Association, but not go too far past the law. Says him and his brother promised to carry you and the boys along for the ride when they took charge of the whole territory the same way they've held power here in Warren County. Is that right?''

"I'm not telling you a damn thing," Bennett declared. Then he turned to Adair. "And you, you son of a bitch, I'll teach you to run your stinking mouth like this."

It was Longarm who answered. "He had a choice, Mikey. He could hang with the rest of you pieces of shit as an accessory to murder. Or he could lay it out for me and be appointed acting sheriff of this county. Guess which one o' them two he chose."

"Bastard."

"Not t' my knowledge," Longarm responded, assuming that he was the one whose parents Bennett was accusing. Of course he could've been wrong about that, in which case he owed Mikey an apology.

"Tell me, Bennett. How are you gonna choose? Roger Donnington decided he'd rather die than face a long term in prison. Got his wish too. How 'bout you, Mikey? Which will it be? That cell back there? Or will you pull your gun and take your chances?''

Bennett wanted to. Longarm could see that. But he was frightened too. Likely he knew how that contest would come out, and he would rather face the years in prison than the certainty of a bullet.

He stood there pale and shaky for what seemed a long time. Then, gingerly and with great deliberation, he unbuckled his belt and let his gun slide down his leg to the floor.

Shortly after Longarm secured Bennett inside his own jail, a shocked and trembling jailer returned from Walker's ranch, where he had rushed to report that Longarm was taking over the county.

"God, I . . . I never seen anything like that. It was awful." The man rushed around behind the sheriff's desk, ignoring Henry Adair, who was already there, and dragged open a bottom drawer. He extracted a whiskey bottle, uncorked it, and took several deep swallows.

"What's awful? Bennett and Daniels being in jail there?" Longarm asked.

The man gave Longarm a strange, haunted look and said, "They are?" as if he hadn't known.

"What were you talking about?"

"Out there. At the judge's place."

"Something happen out there tonight?"

"Yes. It was . . . it was terrible. Just awful, I tell you."

"What?"

"I went out there. You know. To tell the sheriff about you being here and Barry in jail and . . . and everything. And the sheriff, he was out there in the judge's study, them two and that Spanish girl that the judge kept, the three of them setting up late in the night like they was waiting for something."

Longarm grunted. They were all waiting for something, all right. They were waiting for Donnington and the deputies to report back that Longarm was safely dead, that was what they were waiting for. Long damn wait for them too.

"I went in and I told them . . . told them you knew all about what the boys done to those sheepherders . . . and about you being here and Roger and Tim being dead and Barry charged with rape and murder and . . . Mike . . . the sheriff, I mean . . . he jumped up and ran out. Said he was gonna come to town and take care of things. But I guess he didn't. Anyway, the girl. You know the one."

Longarm nodded. He remembered her, all right.

"She jumped up too and got all upset. It was pretty plain she hadn't heard about the murders or the rape. It was the rape of that sheep girl that she kept yelling about. Saying how Walker, he'd promised her the Basques would only be roughed up a little, saying he'd promised they wouldn't none of them get hurt. And she wanted to know all about this girl that was killed and was she really raped, and the judge, he was trying to get her to calm down, trying to tell her that it wasn't his fault, that he'd told the boys to not do any more than beat up the sheep people, but that they'd seen this pretty girl and decided on their own to do more, so it wasn't none of it any fault of his.

"The judge's girlfriend, she started screaming at him. Some language I never heard. Wasn't Spanish either. I know a little Spanish lingo and it wasn't that. This was something else. And when she got done yelling she grabbed up the letter opener from off the judge's desk and she . . . I'm telling you it was terrible. She stabbed him in the belly and she took his pants down and she used the letter opener . . . God, he was still alive when she done it too . . . you know? He was still alive, and she used that dull letter opener to cut his nuts off and his pecker too, and while he was still breathing she stuffed them in his mouth and suffocated him with his own cods. I tell you, I never seen anything like that and I hope to God I never do again."

Longarm stared. The girl had reacted like . . . Jesus.

But then Rodrigo had told him to begin with. The Basques can only be satisfied with blood.

He gathered that they damn sure had been, and not by the blood that he'd spilled.

Come morning, he figured, he would have to get another wire off. To Jorge Luis Rodrigo, this one. Longarm needed to let him know that there was no need now for him to worry and no fear that there would be a war of retribution launched by the Basques.

As for the girl . . . Longarm thought about that too. She'd murdered a man, pure and simple.

But then murder was not, after all, a federal crime. Not part of his jurisdiction at all. No, sir, the correct thing to do here was for him to stay out of this and let the proper territorial officials tend to things after they got here in, oh, another few days or however long it took them to respond.

No, it wouldn't be at all proper for him to go chasing after that murderous young woman.

Longarm relaxed a little, and reached into his pocket for a

cheroot. He figured Billy Vail was gonna be real proud of Longarm's restraint and observation of the jurisdictional niceties this time. Yes, sir, he just figured Billy would say he was doing the right thing here for sure.

Watch for

LONGARM AND THE CHAIN GANG WOMEN

250th novel in the exciting LONGARM series
from Jove

Coming in October!

LONGARM

Explore the exciting Old West with one of the men who made it wild!